THE COCK CROWS MURDER

And Other Tales from the Pulps

WILDSIDE PULP CLASSICS

Murgunstruum and Others, by Hugh B. Cave
Out of the Wreck, by Captain A.E. Dingle
Amazon Nights, by Arthur O. Friel
Satan's Daughter, by E. Hoffmann Price

BY JOHNSTON McCULLEY

Black Star
The Demon
The Man Who Changed Rooms
The Mark of Zorro
The Spider Strain and Other Tales
Tales of Thubway Tham

BY ROBERT E. HOWARD

A Gent from Bear Creek and Other Stories
The Complete Action Stories
Gates of Empire
Graveyard Rats
Treasures of Tartary
Waterfront Fists

PULP MAGAZINE FACSIMILES

The Black Mask #2 (May 1920)
Strange Tales #7 (January 1933)
Ghost Stories (June 1931)
Spicy Mystery Stories (August 1935)
Spicy Mystery Stories (February 1937)
The Phantom Detective #1 (February 1933)

THE MYSTERIOUS WU FANG

The Case of the Suicide Tomb, by Robert J. Hogan

OPERATOR #5

Blood Reign of the Dictator, by Curtis Steele
Death's Ragged Army, by Curtis Steele
Blood Reign of the Dictator, by Curtis Steele
Winged Hordes of the Yellow Vulture, by Curtis Steele

THE COCK CROWS MURDER

And Other Tales from the Pulps

ROBERT LESLIE BELLEM

INTRODUCTION BY DARRELL SCHWEITZER

WILDSIDE PRESS

THE COCK CROWS MURDER
AND OTHER TALES FROM THE PULPS

CONTENTS

ROBERT LESLIE BELLEM:
ROSCOES AND BABES

THERE ARE some writers you read for their subtle depictions of
human character, some for the gripping drive of their narratives,
other for their ideas or intricate plots, but on a few, it can truthfully be
said, are read primarily for their *style*, for the sheer music of their prose.

Robert Leslie Bellem is one such writer. I mean, *listen* to this:

> The sky came down and hit me on the noggin. All the stars in the
> heavens fell with the sky and danced on my optics, and all at once I
> was pitching down a long dark tunnel that gulped me like a raw oys-
> ter. My head floated away. It wasn't my head, it was a balloon, and
> somebody had cut the string. It drifted on a rising current and became
> a whirlpool of pain filled with India ink.
>
> Blooey. I didn't even feel the floor when it bounced me.

That's from "Preview of Murder," *Thrilling Detective*, June 1949,
and as such a relatively late specimen of Bellem's prose — so hardboiled
it sizzles and snaps — the kind of he made famous in *Spicy Mystery* in the
1930s. It's music all right, just not respectable music. More like lively
whorehouse jazz.

Any reader of such fiction knows where we are in the story. S.J.
Perelman, who was fascinated with and amused by Bellem's *Spicy Mystery* fiction, wrote him up in *The New Yorker* in 1938 in a classic article
called, "Somewhere a Roscoe." Perelman commented that Bellem's stories were as ritualized as a bullfight. Indeed they are. We have come to
the part where the tough-guy detective gets hit over the head. A description like the above traditionally follows. Imagine it narrated by an imita-
tion-Bogart voice. Not the real Bogart, who would be more likely to
recite a passage from Dashiell Hammett or Raymond Chandler. While
clearly descended from, at least Hammett (Chandler didn't get started
until Bellem was already roaring along), Bellem never received their
sort of critical acclaim. He's not from the good side of the tracks. *Spicy
Mystery*, not *Black Mask*. You aren't going to be seeing him reprinted in
Library of America any time soon.

More about that ritual. As Perelman notes, in the not-so-loving arms of Dan Turner, Bellem's famous Hollywood detective, is not a particularly safe place. A roscoe (pistol) is likely to "belch 'Chow-chow!'" and then:

> . . . she was as dead as a smoked herring.
> ("Falling Star," September 1936)

> . . . She was dead as vaudeville.
> ("Brunette Bump-Off," May 1938)

It is precisely this verbal inventiveness that makes Bellem entertaining. After a while you *know* what he is going to say. The fun is in the way he says it.

The result reads like a *Mad Magazine* parody of Mickey Spillane written over a decade before anybody had heard of either. Surely this s the very writer to whom the phrase "over the top" should have been applied, if those words had that meaning in his day. And they didn't. "Over the top" in 1938 still referred to soldiers charging out of trenches in World War I. The phrase came to mean rushing into something nasty or difficult from which you can't retreat.

Certainly the average Bellem character charges into his adventure like that. There's no going back.

Yeah, over the top.

Was Bellem kidding? Certainly there is an element of *knowing* parody here. Here was a writer who has having fun. That sense still comes across to the reader. You may not want to read all three thousand stories that Bellem sold to the pulps, but take them a few at a time and they have an undeniable, gaudy glory.

ROBERT LESLIE BELLEM lived between 1902 and 1968. He was a master pulp writer, specializing in the seamier and more sensational sort of pulp fiction. Not for him were the pure-as-the-driven-snow early science fiction magazines, the elegant *Adventure,* or the downright literary *Weird Tales.* (Surprisingly, he had a story in the final issue of *Tales of Magic and Mystery* in 1928.) For one thing, that sort of magazine would not have given full play to Bellem's unusual talents. For another, they didn't pay enough. Like any other working-stiff pulp writer, Bellem went where the dough was, and there was plenty of it in the *Spicy* titles perhaps because added incentive to was necessary to get writers to crank out the sort of stuffed needed to fill the pages of *Spicy Adventure, Spicy Detective, Spicy Mystery,* and *Spicy Western.* These magazines were known, in the slang of the time, as "the hots." They were almost pornography, sold under the counter and taken home in a plain brown wrapper. Of course they were hugely popular and hugely imitated. Even *Weird Tales* began to feature bondage scenes, lesbian whipping scenes, and the like on its covers, but the difference between the other pulps and the *Spicy* line that *Spicy Mystery* or *Spicy Western* actually delivered what their covers promised, what Perelman in *The New Yorker* described as "the sauciest blend of murder and libido this side of Gilles de Rais," further adding, "They have juxtaposed the steely automatic and the frilly panty and found that it pays off."

Indeed it did, to the tune of six to seven cents a word, which meant that for a 4000 word story, probably dashed off in white heat in a couple hours without any revision, a writer could get $240, in an era when a weekly salary might be $15, a new car cost $500, and one might even sometimes live as cheaply as Jack Williamson and Edmond Hamilton did one Depression winter, when they resolved to make a living writing pulp science fiction (which paid nowhere near as well as the *Spicy* magazines) and ended up sharing an off-season cottage in Key West for two dollars *a month*. If a writer could sell just one to just one *Spicy* a month he was sitting pretty. Never mind the formulas. Never mind the need to get the female characters undressed and distressed and somebody messily dead in the "exact, rigid pattern" Perelman noted. $240 dollars was a very good wage.

Bellem did better than a story a month. He wrote for all the *Spicy* line, though he was more likely to be in any given issue of *Spicy Detective* or *Spicy Mystery* than the others. He used pseudonymns, too, Ellery Watson Calder, Harley L. Court, Jerome Severs Perry, John A. Saxon, Harcourt Weems, and perhaps others. Sometimes he had as many as *three* stories in a given issue of *Spicy Mystery,* his natural milieu. He continued throughout the 1940s, as *Spicy Detective* and its companions changed their names to *Speed Detective, Adventure,* and *Western* in a pretense of being less naughty, but mostly in *Dan Turner, Hollywood Detective,* a magazine specially devoted to Bellem's most popular character.

When the pulp era ended, he went to Hollywood, where he continued to find work almost up until his death, writing for such TV shows as *The Lone Ranger, Captain Midnight, Perry Mason, The Iron Horse, 77 Sunset Strip,* and even *Voyage to the Bottom of the Sea.* The 1947 film

Blackmail was based on one of his stories, although he did not write the screenplay.

Bellem was at his best in the mystery field. He wrote two science fiction stories, one each for Ray Palmer's *Amazing* and *Fantastic Adventures*. "Robots Can't Lie" (*Fantastic Adventures* July 1941) is an uninteresting transplant of a detective story into a science fiction setting. Bellem's familiar verbal flair is toned down, though the story begins familiarly enough with a dead dame and words that "burst bomblike" from the hero's "taunt throat." More interesting than the story is the biographical sketch of Bellem in that issue.

He was "predestined" for a writing career, he tells us:

> Ever since I can remember, I've been putting words on paper because I can't help it. But the *kind* of words — action, gunplay, thrills — well, I guess that phase of it was shaped by environment and circumstances.
>
> I recall vividly when I was a grammar school kid in Philadelphia, my home town, where my dad was a railroad dick. I took him his sandwiches that evening and finally located him in the freight yards. He spotted me coming; yelled for me to duck the hell out of the way. I wondered why.
>
> I soon found out. From around the end of a freight car a gun blammed: "Pow!" and my dad staggered; grabbed at his side. Then he regained his balance! sprinted forward. He vanished on the other side of the freight car. Presently he reappeared with a freight thief in tow. Dad had a bullet crease across his ribs. Likewise he had the gun that had done the damage. He also had the trigger artist — and the trigger artist had a busted jaw. Dad was always handy with his fists.

Cops were his heroes, he tells us, and "guys who fought through to victory with their brains backed up by knuckles were supermen; they still are."

But he never became a cop himself. He was a deputy once, during the deadly race riots in Tulsa in 1921. He spent much of his time after that as a reporter and newspaper writer. He had a narrow escape from a collapsing building that fell on his car during an earthquake in Long Beach, California. ("If I hadn't juiced the tripes out of all six cylinders I'd have been a gone goose. Br-r-rr-r!")

While he ended his bio with a promise that he'd write more for *Fantastic Adventures,* he never did. He went back to what he was good at, in what was (or had become) his natural mode of expression.

In other words, Robert Leslie Bellem may have exaggerated a bit, as any storyteller does, but he wrote what he knew.

— Darrell Schweitzer
Philadelphia PA

THE MAN WHO WAS NOT

SLIME. Warm slime. In the darkness, on David Morel's face. Slippery. Wet. Choking him.

Someone was wiping it away, gently. Then Morel knew that it was not slime, It was blood. His own blood.

Abruptly, Morel remembered the dark intersection near his bachelor apartment. The pelting, stinging rain. The speeding, hurtling sedan that had careened around the corner, out of nowhere. The impact as the machine struck him. The sensation of being hurled a great distance through dark emptiness.

And now . . . blood on his face. His own blood. Someone wiping it away. Someone who was familiar, yet a stranger. Someone Morel knew, and yet did not know. Someone whose presence he had often sensed, but whom he had never met.

Morel opened his eyes. Stared at the man who bent over him. The man who was wiping his face. A man he had never seen before.

Then David Morel heard himself speaking. "Your name is LeRom," his voice uttered. Then he wondered why he had said it. Wondered how he had known.

The strange man smiled. "You are right, David Morel. I am LeRom," he answered quietly. His voice was queer. Sinister, yet pleasant. Hypnotically soothing; disturbingly evil.

David Morel looked about him. He was in his own bachelor apartment. On his own bed. Intuitively, he knew Le-Rom had brought him here.

It was midnight. A distant clock tolled out the twelve somber strokes, like hammer-thrusts of doom.

David Morel's head throbbed. He felt strangely light, queerly weightless. There was a confusion to his thoughts. "What happened after that sedan hit "ie?" he asked.

LeRom smiled again. He had a curious smile and pointed, savage teeth. Yet he was oddly handsome. Compelling. He had an animal quality about him. His hands were hairy. David Morel liked him — and hated him. Feared him, rather. LeRom said, "After the sedan struck you, it sped away. Hit-and-run driver. I found you. Picked you up. Brought you home. You're not badly hurt."

David Morel frowned. Everything was very vague, very blurred. He tried to get up from the bed.

LeRom pushed him back. He seemed inhumanly strong. "You need rest," he said. "Go to sleep."

"And you —?"

"I'm going out for a little while."

"But you'll be back, of course. You'll live here." David Morel felt a chill creeping along his spine even as he spoke the words. He didn't know why he had uttered them. Certainly he'd had no intention of inviting LeRom to stay. But there was no other course. LeRom belonged here.

Why?

David Morel did not know. It was damned strange, he thought.

He heard himself saying "Wear one of my suits, LeRom. You have none of your own." He said it even before he was fully aware of the fact that LeRom wore nothing but a raincoat. Now Morel looked, and perceived that he had been correct. Beneath the raincoat, LeRom was naked.

And the raincoat itself belonged to David Morel, Morel had been wearing it when the sedan struck him. Now it clothed LeRom.

LeRom grinned his thanks, wolfishly. When he removed the slicker, David Morel saw that the man's body was very muscular, very hairy. Under the hair, there seemed to be scales . . . foolish, thought Morel . . . but he experienced a crepitant wave of revulsion, repugnance.

LeRom seemed to know his way about Morel's apartment, He found a suit, underwear, socks, shoes, a shirt. He dressed. His movements were curiously light, lithe. He seemed almost to glide across the floor, rather than to walk.

When LeRom had finished dressing, he went to the door of the apartment. His queer eyes were glittering oddly. Lustfully. He was like a beast that had been long caged and now unpent. He departed without a word.

Now that David Morel was alone, he found himself hoping — almost praying — that LeRom would not return. But secretly he knew his hopes to be in vain. LeRom would come back.

Morel shuddered.

Somehow, he felt himself to be in the grip of a fantastic nightmare. Perhaps he had dreamed it all. . . . The hurtling sedan. The scaly, hairy, handsome LeRom who had succored him. . . .

A man like LeRom couldn't really exist, David Morel told himself. No human could emanate such an aura of total, unmitigated evil.

There was one way of finding out.

Morel reached for the telephone beside His bed. He dialed a number. Winifred Carter's number.

As he listened for the ringing signal, he looked at Winifred's picture. The photograph was chastely framed in silver. It rested upon the table alongside Morel's bed. The picture showed a lovely, yellow-haired girl with appealing eyes and kissable lips and full, firm girlish breasts. She was David Morel's fiancee.

Even as he studied her photograph, he heard her voice at the other end of the wire. Drowsy. Husky. Warmly passionate. "Hello?" she said.

"Winifred — beloved!" David Morel whispered.

"Dave — ! What on earth. . . ! Why are you Calling me at such an ungodly hour, darling?"

"I — I think I've been dreaming. Having nightmares. I had to talk to you. Had to hear your voice. Had to ask you a question." Morel said it swiftly, tensely.

"What question, Dave?" the girl's tone sounded abruptly troubled.

"Did — did I visit you tonight?"

"But of course," her relieved laughter tinkled liquidly. "Don't tell me you'd forgotten! You just left, less than an hour ago."

"I was . . . normal when I left you?"

"Normal? Why, of course, silly! Normal . . . and very sweet!"

"I was alone?"

"Alone? What do you mean?"

"When I left you, there was nobody with me? No other man?"

"No. There was no one with you."

"And I kissed you? Held you in my arms?"

"Dave!" she drew a sharp breath. "Suppose someone were listening on the wire?"

"But — I did those things?"

"Y-yes," she confessed reluctantly, sweetly. "And now go back to sleep, darling. Get some rest."

David Morel hung up, slowly. Then he'd really visited Winifred Carter that evening. That much was no dream, no hallucination. But the events which had followed. . . . Maybe they'd been part of a nightmare . . . ?

He got up from his bed. He was clad, he perceived, in fresh

pajamas. He looked at himself in a mirror.

He went white.

There was blood on the front of his pajama jacket. Fresh blood. His own blood.

"Then . . . I was struck by that sedan!" he whispered harshly.

And in that case, he knew LeRom really existed. Had brought him here to the apartment, after the accident. And would return, evilly. . . .

"He can't come back! He mustn't!" David Morel muttered to himself. "I must find him and tell him to go away!"

He slipped out of his pajamas. Got dressed. Went out into the rain-whipped night.

He seemed curiously light on his feet. Walking was oddly effortless; ridiculously easf. It required no exertion . . .

. . . Almost it required no volition. David Morel found himself heading straight toward the waterfront district. He did not know why. He was aware of only one thing: he would find LeRom near the water-front. It was as if he were bound to LeRom with invisible ties —

He heard a scream. A woman's harsh, shrieking cry of fear and of tortured agony.

David Morel broke into a loping run.

Sweat streamed into his eyes. Cold sweat He rounded a corner in the rain. His muscles crawled on his bones, like live worms. . . . He brought up short.

A girl lay in the gutter. A girl of the night, pathetic in her rouge and her jaded, cheap finery. Her dress had been savagely ripped from her form; her brassiere, her tissue-thin panties were torn into dangling rib-bons, so that David Morel could see the claw-marks on her breasts and her thighs. . . .

The claw-marks were bleeding. And the girl was struggling wildly, helplessly, in the grasp of a hovering, slavering creature who pawed her, mauled her, tortured her with fist-blows and ripping, lacerating teeth . . .

The creature was LeRom.

David Morel leaped at the man; pounced on his back; bore him to the freshet-running gutter. Held LeRom's face under the muddy water until the man choked and gasped and went suddenly limp.

Then Morel released his grip.

LeRom staggered to his feet. He was smiling. Suave. He looked at David Morel and said, "Another time, you will not stop me." Then he took Morel's arm. "Let's go home," he said.

David Morel nodded. His loathing, his disgust for the bestial LeRom were not strong enough to permit him to argue. Because his liking for the hairy, handsome man was stronger than his hate.

Together they loped through the storm, leaving the bleeding girl there in the gutter, moaning.

BACK in David Morel's apartment, LeRom grinned vulpinely. "You know what to do," he said in a quiet voice.

Morel nodded and went to the telephone. He dialed the operator. "Get me police headquarters," he said.

In a moment, an authoritative voice said, "Central Station."

"This is David Morel, My apartment has been ransacked." Morel gave his address.

"We'll send a man," the voice answered swiftly.

Morel hung up. He saw that LeRom was busy pulling out drawers, upsetting their contents on the floor; opening closets and dumping out clothing in a chaotic heap.

The doorbell rang.

LeRom's face contorted savagely. He glided into the kitchenette; secreted himself in the dumb-waiter shaft.

And David Morel went to the front door, trembling. He opened it.

Two uniformed bluecoats were standing there. They looked grim, forbidding. One of them spoke. "Your name David Morel?"

Morel nodded.

"You're under arrest lor attacking a woman on Front Street."

David Morel stiffened his shoulders. "You're crazy. I haven't been near Front Street in days," he lied.

"We found a pocketbook'. Yours."

Morel laughed. "It was stolen from me. My apartment was robbed tonight, during my absence. I've already reported it to headquarters."

The uniformed officer frowned. And then, abruptly, a plain-clothes detective came up the stairs. The detective pushed his way forward. "This the apartment that was ransacked?" he demanded.

Morel nodded. "Yes. And these other officers tell me a woman was attacked, down by the waterfront. The attacker dropped a billfold. Mine."

The plain-clothes detective smiled. "Good thing you reported the burglary. Otherwise you might be suspected of being the attacker yourself. Well look over the apartment; see if the burglar left any dues."

David Morel nodded. "Come in," he said.

Fifteen minutes later, the police departed. When they had gone, Morel went into the kitchenette and opened the shaft of the dumbwaiter. LeRom stepped from his concealment. He was smiling. "You carried it off very nicely," I he said.

Morel felt suddenly sick, nauseated. He had lied to the police; had saved this bestial LeRom from arrest. Why?

He didn't know.

But he did know that LeRom's hold on him was now stronger than before. And that LeRom's evil aura was also stronger, more pronounced. It was as though David Morel's He had added to his strange visitor's stature . . .

Suddenly, David Morel picked up a kitchen chair, raised it high over his head, brought it smashing down on LeRom's evil skull. LeRom uttered no sound. He slumped unconscious at Morel's feet, crushed under the berserk fury of Morel's unexpected attack.

M orel stared down at the fallen man. Saw that the descending chair had torn a gaping-wound in LeRom's forehead.

But the wound did not bleed!

David Morel turned and hurled himself out of the apartment, his soul filled with a great and nameless dread.

Hatless in the rain, he pelted through the storm as though seeking to flee from the influence of a sinister calamity that hovered over him . . . As he ran, he thought of that girl who LeRom had beaten and bitten and clawed . . .

A vast pity for her seized him. In some manner, David Morel felt himself responsible for the sadistic cruelty, the harm that had befallen her. He must make amends, he told himself . . .

He found an all-night lunchroom, a public phone. Dialed police headquarters. Got the girl's address. Her name. He went out again.

He found the house where she lived. A shoddy hotel of ill repute. To the pimply clerk he said, "Where is Margie Knipp's room?"

"Second floor. 214 — to the left of the stairs."

David Morel went up.

He rapped softly on the door of Room 214. It opened.

Morel stared into the bruised, strained features of a girl — an auburn-haired girl who might have been beautiful, once. Now there were marks of dissipation around her eyes, her mouth. And her face was purled, lacerated . . .

She wore a thin kimono. Through the sleazy garment, David Morel could see the pallid whiteness of her flesh, the marks of bruising fists . . . and the impressions of teeth — human teeth — LeRom's teeth! The brands were upon her thighs and upon her soft woman-breasts . . .

She was staring at David Morel, as though he were an apparition. She turned corpse-pallid. "God!" she sobbed; and would have slammed her door in MoreFs face.

But he thrust his foot forward, so that the portal would not dose. He smiled at her. "I mean you no harm, Margie Knipp," he said gently.

"You told me that before!" she choked. "And then . . . you beat me!"

David Morel frowned. The girl, of course, was suffering from a delusion, he told himself. LeRom had attacked her, there on that dark street near the waterfront. And Morel had intervened — saved her from LeRom's maniacal fury. Now she had the two men confused. She was under the impression that it was David Morel who had beaten her . . .

Morel said, "No. I didn't hurt you, my dear. I pulled that other man away from you. I saved you from him."

She stared at him, wide-eyed. "Are you mad?" she panted. "It was you who jumped on me. There was no other man."

David Morel's thoughts were momentarily blurred into a hazy confusion. For a single instant, he almost believed the girl to be telling the truth. There came to him a nauseous sensation that she was right; that it had been he himself — David Morel — who had beaten and clawed and punched and bitten her . . . It seemed as though he could still almost taste the salt tang of her blood in his mouth . . . the soft resilient breasts under his battering fists . . .

And then the feeling passed. David Morel smiled. "I came to make amends for what that other man did to you," he said softly. He reached into his pocket, extracted a roll of bills.

The girl's eyes widened avariciously. "Come in," she bade him. She smiled — a hard, professional, meaningless smile; a smile intended to be coquettish, provocative, inviting . . .

Morel entered her room, closed the door behind him; locked it. He handed two twenties to the girl.

Somehow, her acceptance of the money seemed to ease David Morel's conscience. He wondered why. Wondered why he should feel so much responsibility for the sadistic actions of the hairy, scaly LeRom.

The girl tucked the two twenties into her shoe. Leaning over, she permitted her kimono to fall open in front. Morel perceived that she wore nothing beneath the garment. No step-ins; no brassiere. Her breasts were soft, downward-pointing cones. Her body, save for the bruises, the scratches, the teeth-marks, was white and flawless and intriguing.

She saw Morel studying her femininity. She smiled again — a hard, studied smile. "You're not such a bad egg after all," she said in a tone meant to be light.

"I wanted to repay you for what . . . happened to you, earlier tonight," he told her earnestly. And meant it from the bottom of his soul. Then, abruptly, a strange feeling swept over him. It was a sensation of evil — a gnawing, festering, cancerous evil that grew within him, stifling his pity for the girl; replacing pity with . . . desire . . . !

He tried to fight it down. He had never had commerce with women like Margie Knipp. But now, the sight of her bared breasts, her white thighs, her lush hips, seemed to ignite a bestial flame within him. Seemed to give life to a new-born demon that possessed his veins and his mind and his consciousness.

Through the room's locked door, he heard a voice, whispering. A slithery, evil voice. The voice of . . . LeRom! LeRom was saying "Don't be a damned fool, David Morel! Make love to the girl. You've paid her forty dollars. She expects you to . . . kiss her, at least!"

And David Morel obeyed, because he could not help himself. Obeyed, because LeRom's word was law. Obeyed, because he was floundering and engulfed in LeRom's evil aura, which penetrated the locked door like a noxious, fetid fog — an evil miasma of confused malig-nance against which he cotild not fight . . .

He leaped at the girl.

She had grown suddenly white-faced. "God — don't look at me . . . that way!" she moaned.

David Morel grabbed her, crushed her against himself. He pushed aside the kimono; pressed her, trembling, quivering body against him. His fingers bit into the soft flesh of her throbbing breasts, so that she choked out a cry of agony. He muffled her cry under the savage impact of his bruising kiss.

She squirmed, helplessly. And the undulant movements of her body set David Morel's blood afire. She was soft and warm. Her breasts were pliant, silken, spongy. Morel balled his fists and struck her on the hips. The thighs.

And all the time he struck her, he had the queer sensation that he was not hirri-self. He was — LeRom!

But that was insanity. LeRom was out in the corridor — outside the locked door, LeRom had some sort of hypnotic, malign influence over David Morel. LeRom was compelling Morel to do bestial, sadistic things to the auburn-haired Margie Knipp . . .

Suddenly Morel regained control over himself. He opened his eyes; discovered that he had thrown the auburn-haired girl upon the divan, and was pinning her down with his weight . . . She had fainted; was offering no resistance. . . .

David Morel's mouth opened. A harsh, sobbing oath issued from his dry throat. "God — what have I done?" he gibbered frantically. It was as if scales had fallen from his eyes, so that he could view his own incomprehensible bestiality.

An icy, frigid fear filled him. Had he killed the girl? His hand went to her left breast; pressed deep. He felt.the fluttering of her heart. She was alive . . .

"Thank God!" David Morel whispered.

And then he thought of LeRom, outside the door. LeRom, who had forced him to this foul misdeed. An abrupt bitterness filled David Morel; a bitterness that turned suddenly to frantic, insane hate. He would kill LeRom —

He whirled, sped to the door, unlocked it, threw it wide.

LeRom was standing there, grinning evilly.

David Morel gazed at the man. Saw the bloodless wound on LeRom's forehead, where he had smashed the man down with a kitchen chair, not so long ago.

The wound was almost completely healed!

"You — you foul fiend from hell!" Morel snarled. "You've made me — attack this girl! And now shell turn me over to the police. Ill be arrested — jailed —"

LeRom grinned again, "There's a way out," he said quietly.

"A . . . way out?"

"Yes. I'll kill her. Then she won't be able to talk."

Horror surged through the crevices of David Morel's soul. He cringed. "You'd . . . kill her . . . ?"

"Why not? She's just a common bum. She's better off dead." LeRom strode — glided, rather — past David Morel, into the auburn-haired prostitute's room. He leaned over the girl. Licked her naked body with gleaming eyes. His hairy hands clawed toward her throat.

David Morel sobbed out a curse. "Damn you — let her alone!" he grated. He flung himself at LeRom.

Strangely, the hairy, scaly man offered little resistance. He seemed weary, fatigued, without strength. One blow of Morel's fist sent him sprawling, unconscious.

Morel picked him up, lugged him out of the room, down a rear stairway, into the rain-swept street. LeRom's sagging form was very light; very easy to carry.

Out of the leaden sky, a tongue of lightning forked. The weeping clouds unleashed a torrent of spewing rain that danced, dervish-like, on the black mirror of the pavement. Thunder rumbled ominously.

David Morel heard the thock-thock-thock of tire-chains on an approaching taxi; saw the machine's headlights. A weird idea gripped him. He waited until the cab swung around the corner toward him. And then —

With a vicious sweep, he hurled Le-Rom's limp body from him, into the street, straight under the wheels of the speeding machine.

It was horrible.

The spinning wheels impacted against LeRom's form. Twisted the man's evil body into a grotesque shapelessness. Crunched LeRom's bones, split open his abdomen so that bloodless viscera was squeezed out, nauseously . . .

David Morel retched and was very sick. Wide-eyed, he saw the taxi speeding away, not stopping to ascertain what it had struck. And then, suddenly, he heard the shrill blasting bleat of a police whistle from the far, dark corner . . . And the pelting of heavy, running feet . . .

"God!" Morel whispered. "The police!"

It was then that stark, frenetic terror struck its fangs into David Morel's congealed marrow. He had killed a man. He was a murderer. He had slain? Le-Rom; and he would hang for it. . . ! Because the authorities would not take into account LeRom's malignant evil. They would not realize that Morel had done the world a favor of ridding the earth of that foul, obscene, hair-scaly creature . . . They would know only that David Morel had murdered LeRom — and because of it, Morel would hang by fee neck until he was dead . . .

Almost he could feel the trap yawning open abruptly beneath his feet; could feel the noose tightening about his throat; could experience the neefc-snapping jerk as he reached the end of the rope mid dangled, choking, over nothingness . . .

He turned and ran, blindly, in the rain.

The lightness, the weightlessness, was gone from him now. His feet were heavy, leaden, dragging. It was the nightmare experience that he had sometimes known in his dreams — the sensation of trying to run, to escape deadly pursuit; only to find his muscles disobedient, his legs tethered by some unseen, gripping tentacles that impeded him and slowed him and held him back . . .

Perspiration bathed David Morel's forehead, streamed from his armpits, soaked through his underwear to meet the moisture of the rain that drenched him from without. Blindly, insanely, wildly, he pelted through the night, while time stood still and space was not. Was he outdistancing his pursuers? He dared not look back to see. He knew only that he must go on . . . and on . . . and on . . . toward some unknown haven, some unthought-of refuge . . .

Sanctuary . . . Where would he find it? And then, suddenly, he knew.

He knew, because his laggard footsteps had brought him to the house where lived his fiancée, Winifred Carter.

Into the lobby of the apartment he plunged, desperately, like a man bereft of reason, stripped of everything except the blind, unreasoning, animal desire for self-preservation. Dimly in his consciousness glowed a far-away gleam of light . . . and he knew that it was the light of Winifred Carter's love . . .

Her lqve . . . and her purity t She might save him; might cloak him in the gentle, enfolding concealment of her sweet, virginal womanhood. . . . At least, in her arms* he would know a few brief moments of respite from the warped and numbing horror that was gibbering at his heels.

He reached her door. Knocked importunately, desperately.

The door opened, after long ages.

David Morel looked into Winifred Carter's lovely blue eyes. Saw the surprised, startled wonderment that grew in her gaze. "Dave — what's wrong?" she whispered tensely. There was something about Morel's haggard face that must have filled her with sudden fear.

"Quick — for God's sake —" he gasped out thickly. "Let me in — hide me!"

"Hide you? From what —?"

"The — the police! I've . . . just . . . killed a man —"

She blanched — and drew him swiftly into the apartment; closed the door; locked it with desperate haste. And then, became she loved David Morel, she took him into her arms . . .

She wore only a thin, gossamer nightgown, cut very low in front; and she pressed Morel close, so that he could feel the warmth of her two swelling breasts, felt the quivering of her body, the throbbing of her bosoms, the sweetly-arched curves of her hips . . . Then it was that her woman-fragrance, her feminine body, aroused a dormant, evil desire within David Morel's soul . . .

. . . A desire for her that he had never before known. A bestiality that swept over him like a riptide, carrying him out into a dark sea of unclean passion . . . Abruptly it seemed as though David Morel were once more under the malign, sinister, demoniac influence of LeRom — Winifred Carter's blue eyes widened. Morel's hands were in her golden hair, twisting, entwining . . . He had pulled her nightgown over her shoulders, baring her breasts. He was cupping those sweetly-firm mounds, sinking his fingers deep. . . . "Dave — Dave — what are you . . . doing. . . ?" she gasped out, in a stricken, horrified whisper.

Then, before Morel could respond, he felt hard hands at his shoulders; heard a Mephistophelean, sardonic laugh behind him. He was being pulled backward, off-balance . . .

He turned, struggled in the triumphant grasp of his captor. He stared into the gleaming, hell-lustrous fiend's eyes of — LeRom!

"You thought you could kill me, David Morel. But I am above death. I am LeRom — and I am deathless!" the scaly, hairy, handsome man mocked him.

Twin emotions surged through David Morel's seething soul. One was an emotion of relief — because LeRom was not dead. He had not killed the man; therefore he was not a murderer. But the relief he felt was swiftly drowned in a flooding fear that sapped his sanity.

LeRom was alive — and his triumpham evil was a goading, mocking reality.

LeRom raised his fist, struck More in the face.

Morel sank to the floor. And sagging semi-conscious, he saw LeRom spring at Winifred Carter!

She screamed. Her cry was drownec out by LeRom's guttural laughter. LeRom had her in his hairy arms. LeRorr had ripped her silken gown from her body. Her virginal form was revealed, Her perfect breasts, her white torso, her lilting hips and thighs and legs . . . LeRom was laving her curves with his hands; was kissing her mouth, her throat, her shoulders. He was drawing her more tightly into his arms. . .

It took every ounce of David Morel's energy to stagger to his feet. Then, blindly, drunkenly, he hurled himself at the man he hated. Flung himself at LeRom.

Fists battering, mouth twisting under writhing curses, Morel assailed the man, fighting with an atavistic fury born of ancestors who lived by teeth and claws . . . The berserk rage of his attack caught LeRom unprepared. The evil one released his grasp upon Winifred Carter, and she swayed forward, crouched in a corner while the two men fought. Fought savagely, horribly. David Morel could feel LeRom's hot breath in his face, like a fetid anaesthetic, choking him. He whimpered, and smashed his knotted fist into LeRom's snarling teeth. LeRom staggered; and then he lashed out with his foot, caught Morel in the groin. Lancing spates of agony gushed through David Morel's soul. He choked back the sick hell that filled him. Choked it back, and flung himself once more at his enemy. They came to grips.

Morel could hear LeRom's evil voice in his ear. "You cannot kill me, David Morel! I am deathless — because all evil is deathless. And I am the evil that dwells in your own soul!"

Morel recoiled, horrified. Then, suddenly, he knew . . . he knew!

LeRom — LeRom was David Morel himself! Lerom was Morel spelled backward! Through some foul necromancy, LeRom — who was not a man, but who was only the evil side of David Morel's own nature — had found life; had found separate existence!

"God in heaven! *I* am not one man, but two!" David Morel sobbed wildly. . . . And then he understood why he had liked LeRom even while hating and fearing him. Understood the ties that had bound him to LeRom. Comprehended the monstrous psychic liaison that existed between LeRom and himself. . . !

He was on the floor, battling desper-ately with LeRom now. Was clawing and scratching and gouging and pummeling. Oblivious to the blows and kicks that LeRom rained on him, he fought grimly, with the fury of desperation. Fought on, knowing that if he failed, he would die . . . and the evil of LeRom would live. . . . And if that happened, LeRom would take Winifred Carter, bend her to his will, break her soul and her body on the rack of his lust and his demoniac passions . . .

"You fiend! You won't . . . do that!" David Morel grated through blood-dribbling lips. And he renewed the savage fury of his battle. "You . . . shall not . . . have Winifred!" he sobbed. "I . . . love her! I'll save her from you!"

Even as he spoke, LeRom seemed to grow weaker. The utter fiendishness of his face glowed like a noxious hell-light. David Morel felt the strength flowing from his antagonist's sinews . . . and it seemed to be seeping into his own veins! Renewed, his courage leaped back into his soul, and Morel tasted the sweetness of approaching triumph.

Approaching triumph . . . impending victory . . . But God! At what cost. As Morel closed his fingers about LeRom's throat and throttled the breath of life from the evil one's gullet, it seemed, suddenly, as though he were choking himself; as though he were cutting off his own breath. Abruptly, a hellish pain cascaded through David Morel . . .

A woman's pains of parturition, of child-birth, could not have equalled this sudden agony, Morel thought dully. Because he was not giving birth. . . . To the contrary, he was absorbing LeRom into his own body, his own recoiling, revolting, rebellious soul!

The struggle sickened him, maddened him until he screamed with the savage torture. Screamed — and yet uttered no sound, as a man screams soundlessly in the throes of nightmare. And then, suddenly, it was over . . .

LeRom had disappeared.

And in the moment of his triumphant victory over evil, David Morel lost consciousness . . . Did not know that Winifred Carter had crept to him, cradled his bloody head against her snowy breasts.

D AVID MOREL awakened to the clean hospital-smell of a private room in a quiet sanitarium. A nurse leaned over him.

He looked at her. "Where . . . am . . . I?" he whispered.

"Sh-h-h," she answered. "You must be very still, very quiet. You were struck by a hit-and-run driver last night. You're in St. Luke's Hospital. You're badly hurt, but you'll recover."

He closed his eyes and slept. Ages later, when once more he was awake, he found Winifred Carter seated beside his bed.

"Winifred — beloved!" he gasped. He grasped at her hand, clung to it. "Tell me — was it all a nightmare? Was I merely hit by a car? Did I dream all those other things? LeRom, and . . . that fight in your apartment. . . ?"

She looked at him oddly. Her eyes were shining, "As far as the world will ever know, it was just hallucination, my sweet!" she whispered gently. "But —"

"But what?"

"But I know what happened!" she answered him. "I saw . . . LeRom! And you bested him! You have conquered your evil side, Dave darling. And when you have recovered . . ."

She blushed, hesitant to speak of the happiness that lay in store for them both. But David Morel knew, and was content.

ENOUGH GLORY

LOS ANGELES, Aug. 5 (UP) — District Attorney Buron Fitts said today he had obtained evidence that several murders have been committed on the Pacific Coast in the course of Communist party infiltration activities. He said the evidence would be presented to a grand jury tomorrow.

— Dispatch in the *New York Times*
August 6, 1940

H E HAD a hunch there'd be trouble tonight. Men getting hurt: himself among them, maybe. He advanced on the platform. The hall hummed with an electrical tension he could feel almost physically, like a warning touch. It was something to make you afraid if you were a coward. Or to make you all the more steadfast if you believed in your message, as Shell Macklin did.

His friend Dave Obrowski from the stockroom of the Amalgamated Motors plant was introducing him. Doing a loud job of it. A little too loud:

"Our next speaker is a man we all know and respect. Nobody could call him un-American; his father fought in the war to save democracy. He's been in the machine tool division of Amalgamated Motors eight loyal years . . ."

Shell Macklin frowned. He didn't like this preamble. It sounded too much like an apology for him. And he needed no apologies for what he had to say. This was America. A man had a right to talk if he wanted to. That was the meaning of free speech, wasn't it?

He felt like a green boxer climbing into the ring. Jittery. There were a lot of strangers in the crowded hall; fellows he didn't recognize. Beefy lugs who muttered among themselves. They looked like cops. Or hired gunhands.

Obrowski kept talking. ". . . been a laboring man all his life. He knows the laboring man's problems. He loves the United States as much as we all do, but . . ."

There it was again. Apology. Fear. Maybe Obrowski sensed the same tension Shell Macklin felt. And Obrowski was a little fellow with a limp earned in a shop accident. Not much use in a fight. Even a guy with two good legs and two good dukes would need a lot of moxie to tangle with those bruisers in the first few rows.

Obrowski finally ran down: "I give you that patriot and worker for the Cause, Shell Macklin." He stepped back.

Macklin took the center and waited a moment for the beginning applause. It was thin, scattered. More booing than cheers. He had the jitters again.

It was tough enough to make your first speech to a friendly audience; but these catcalls gave him stage fright. A big, bald man in the front row said: "Sit down, you lousy Red."

That did it. Macklin lost his nervousness. Anger was what he had needed. Now he had it. He put thunder in his voice. "We've got hecklers with us, fellows. That's okay with me. Maybe they'll learn something."

Somebody whistled encouragement.

He said: "I'm no speaker. But I know what I feel. What I believe. I know we're living under a corrupt and outmoded form of government that needs changing."

The big man with the bald head made a raucous noise with his lips. His eyebrows were thick patches of unmowed black lawn that came together in a single line. "You stinking yellow bum!"

Macklin spoke directly to him. "You say I'm yellow because I'm against the System. Because I want to throw off my chains. I say I'm as good a patriot as you. Maybe better."

"Oh, yeah?"

Macklin's mouth straightened. "At least I don't believe in manufacturing murder machinery so a privileged few can fatten their pockets the way Amalgamated is doing. Six months of tooling for production of airplane engines.

"For America, they tell us. For Europe and profit, I say. So bombers can drop their eggs on women and kids."

The bald man said: "Why don't you quit your job if you feel that way about it?"

"I am. Tomorrow. From now on I'm putting in my time telling the masses what suckers they are."

"You heel!" the bald man snarled. "You're quitting because Amalgamated would fire you when they see where you stand."

Macklin said: "Sure they'd fire me. But that's not why I'm quitting. I —"

"How much do you get from Moscow for stirring up trouble, rat?"

the bald man taunted.

Macklin was stung. The question was unfair. "Our Party has no connection with Moscow!" He hotly parroted the answer he'd been taught. "It's as much a part of this country as the Democrats or the Republicans.

"But when the workers get wise to themselves there won't be any more Democrats or Republicans. Or airplane motors for murderers. Or slaves killing themselves to make rich men richer. Or hired hecklers like you!"

That was when the bald man pulled a blackjack and made for him. Others followed. Workers and party members saw what was starting. They rushed the troublemakers. Chairs splintered. Back in the hall a woman screamed.

Dave Obrowski gasped: "Riot!" He limped toward the wings. Macklin didn't notice. He was staring toward the source of that feminine cry.

"Peggy!" he said, feeling for the first time the chill of sudden fear. "Peggy!"

Peggy Ryan — the girl who might even now have been his wife if her father — but what was the use? She was struggling to reach the platform: yellow hair flying, blue eyes terrified.

Macklin's heart leaped with elation to know she cared enough for him to seek him out here. Then, with sickening reaction, he realized that she herself was in peril: being buffeted, crushed. Unhesitatingly he lunged toward the platform's edge.

The big bald man with the black eyebrows blocked him. "I've been hoping for this," he grunted. He swung his blackjack.

Macklin side-stepped, took the blow on his shoulder. It hurt plenty even there. His left arm felt numb. He slugged a fist at the bald man — and connected.

Now the hall was boiling. There must have been more toughies planted in the audience than Macklin suspected. The workers had their hands full. Chair legs thunked on skulls. Men went down. Macklin ducked another blackjack smash.

Behind him there was the sudden sharp splat of gunfire; a whimpering moan. Macklin turned. He saw crippled little Dave Obrowski toppling, shot through the brain. A sob swelled in Macklin's throat. "You cowards! You cold-blooded murderers!"

The bald guy's blackjack caught him across the mouth. He felt splinters coming off his teeth, blood gushing. His lips were wet sponges.

The bald man hit him again.

Over the roaring in his ears Macklin heard siren-whine. Somebody yowled: "Cops!"

It was all confused and drunken. The bald man was scuttling to an exit, his plug-uglies following. It was like a movie being unreeled too fast. Even Dave Obrowski's corpse on the platform seemed more like a wax dummy than a man.

Everything was blurry; nothing real. Except Peggy Ryan.

She was real enough. She was close to the stage now: her dress torn, her eyes wild. "Shell, darling!"

He went down the three wooden steps to her. His shirt was all blood, and his mouth hurt terribly. He tried to talk but the words were thick and moist, like gruel.

Peggy pulled him. He stumbled along, blindly. In a dim way he knew she got him out of the hall ahead of the riot squad. He knew he was in her car, cutting through the night. The wind was good on his face, like a poultice.

SHE parked on a side street and mopped the blood from his lips with a handkerchief. "Shell! Thank God you're all right! Thank God I got you away before the police came!"

"Cops got nothing on me."

"They'd have taken your name as a witness. Amalgamated would have fired you —"

"Can't fire me. I'm quitting. You heard me say it." His fists closed around a promise of vengeance. "They'll pay for killing Obrowski. I'll make them pay."

"Shell, darling. Listen to me. Will you listen, Shell?"

He nodded, knowing what she was going to say. Arguments. Always arguments. She didn't realize how he felt about things. She didn't understand.

"Shell. You can't go on this way. Some night you'll be killed . . ."

He thought of Dave Obrowski. "Other men have been killed. Other men maimed. There's always suffering where imperialistic wars are to be fought. But the time's coming when Capital will sing another tune."

She shivered. "You're talking like Hitler, Shell — his fight against Western capitalism, and all that. You're decent to the core, but you're all mixed up."

That wasn't Peggy talking, he told himself. It was her father, old Senator Ryan. The preacher of preparedness; the man who wouldn't let his daughter marry Macklin — because he distrusted Macklin's comrades.

Macklin said: "Capitalism pulled the trigger on Dave Obrowski. Hired thugs of the warmongers who would help England. They think they can beat us to our knees that way."

"Shell —"

"But they can't. For every worker they kill, ten will rise. Only we won't fight with bullets. We'll use reason. Maybe you'd call it revolution. But a bloodless one. Then this country will belong to the men who made it. The masses."

Peggy's eyes were wet. "You really believe that, don't you? It isn't glory you want. You're sincere. But you can't see you're being used by fifth columnists to weaken your own government for attack by some foreign dictatorship —"

Her father's words again. Not hers. Macklin got out of the car. "When you can forget your father's propaganda, send for me." He strode off, his heart as bruised as his battered lips.

He damned himself for loving a girl who belonged to the class it was his duty to hate. Why couldn't she understand that he was as loyal to his country as any other American? Except that his loyalty was for the downtrodden. The people who really were the United States!

There was a messenger waiting for him at his boarding house. Macklin was wanted at Party headquarters right away. "Soon as I clean up the blood," he said.

All four of the local bigwigs were there when he arrived. "Sit down, Shell. You took a drubbing tonight." That was Jack Lanneran talking. Bluff, hearty Jack Lanneran. Party whip and all-around good guy. A man you could trust. A man who'd share his last dime with you.

Macklin said: "I'm okay. I'm alive. Obrowski isn't."

"Your friend, wasn't he, Shell?"

"My friend. Yes." Macklin's knuckles showed white.

"We've been wondering how those company thugs found out about the meeting so they could break it up. Somebody talked. You didn't, did you?"

"I didn't tell anybody but Peggy —"

The words were out before he could stop them. He said swiftly: "She's my girl. She wouldn't tell. I'd swear that."

"It doesn't matter now. You can't bring Obrowski back with words."

"You can't bring him back with anything," Macklin said.

"He can be avenged, though."

"How?"

"By finishing a job he thought up. This was it." They tossed a type-written paper at Macklin.

Queer. Macklin hadn't known Obrowski could use a typewriter. Hadn't known he could even write English. You can't always tell about a guy, Macklin thought. He read the paper.

It was suggested that certain figures be altered on the final specifications for machine tools which Amalgamated intended to use in changing over its plant for the production of airplane engines. Then the tools would be of incorrect pattern — but not too noticeably so. Especially if approved on inspection by someone in authority.

A micrometrically haywire bore here. A misplaced measurement there. Not enough to show. But when engine manufacture started, the sabotage would pop up.

Pistons wouldn't fit cylinder blocks on the assembly line. Gears would fail to mesh. Instead of producing motors, Amalgamated would be turning out junk.

That would mean new tooling again! Starting from scratch, fabricating substitute patterns, correctly designed this time. Six months of delayed production; six months of war-profiteering shot to pieces was the way it read.

Macklin looked up. "Well?"

"It's been approved. By Comrade Rostoff himself. From New York. He's in town. Just got here. What do you say, Shell?"

Macklin frowned. "Why should I have anything to say?"

"You're in charge of the machine tool division. You're the only one who could change those specifications and okay the jobs on final inspection. It'd be up to you."

A funny feeling hit him in the stomach. Talking was one thing. Being beaten up, yes. But sabotaging Amalgamated property . . .

"I don't know," he mumbled.

"What is there to know? Obrowski was your friend. A helpless cripple. They killed him. Blackjacked you. Are you scared to hit back?"

"Not scared. No."

"Well, then. It's not like you're shedding anybody's blood. You'd be shedding their dollars and that'd hurt them worse. Maybe make them realize they can't murder workers without paying. That's the way Comrade Rostoff sees it."

Rostoff. Big shot from New York. The man whose editorials told you how this country was being made a sucker by England. The man who believed in letting Europe work out its own destiny, as being no concern of ours.

"I'll think it over," Macklin said.

Jack Lanneran got up. "Sure. Let's take a walk, Shell. We'll iron it out."

Walking, Macklin fumbled for words to explain his indecision. Peggy Ryan couldn't have told her father about the meeting, so he could have it broken up in a riot. In a way, that would have made her responsible for what happened to Obrowski.

She wouldn't do a thing like that. She wouldn't be a partner to murder.

"She wouldn't be a partner to sabotage either," he said aloud.

"Who wouldn't?" Jack Lanneran asked him.

"My girl. If I went through with this deal and she found it out, I'd lose her."

Lanneran said: "Then don't let her know."

That made it seem furtive, underhanded. It would always be on his conscience, like a barrier between himself and the girl he loved. "I'm all muddled up," he muttered.

"Maybe the blackjacking," Lanneran said. "You took enough to make anybody a little punchy. Tell me what's eating you. Maybe I can straighten you out."

"This sabotage thing. Would I be pulling it for revenge because I got slugged? Because Obrowski was killed? Personal motives haven't got any place in a man's wanting to help his country. It's the country itself that counts. The workers."

Lanneran's voice was quietly persuasive. "You'd be doing it for them, keeping them out of saber-rattling that leads to war. This armament for defense — what have we got to defend? From whom?"

Somehow, at that moment, it sounded glib and rehearsed.

Macklin dismissed the glibness. He had his own problems. Changing those specifications would be treachery to a firm that had employed him at decent wages eight long years. Treachery to everything Peggy Ryan believed in.

Lanneran said urgently: "A man's got to make some sacrifice for the Cause. Obrowski even sacrificed his life. You're not being asked to go that far. Chances are you won't be caught. You won't lose this Peggy

Ryan."

He looked up. "Here we are back at Party headquarters. Let's go in and tell the boys you're going through with it."

"Okay." Shell Macklin shrugged, made his decision. "Let's tell them." He and Lanneran entered the building.

THE rear room's door was ajar. The bigwigs were back there. Talking to somebody whose voice sounded curiously familiar. Somebody they addressed as Comrade Rostoff.

Lanneran looked suddenly upset. "Don't go in there, Shell. Not just yet." He tried to draw Macklin away.

But Macklin had already caught a glimpse of the man with the familiar voice. The man they called Rostoff.

Rostoff was big; beefy. His head was bald. His eyebrows were black patches of unmowed lawn. He was the guy who had hit Shell Macklin across the mouth with a blackjack.

For a moment it didn't make sense. Then, slowly, it did. There was only one possible explanation. Macklin shook himself away from Lanneran's grasp. "Let go of me. I'll kill the heel."

"Nix, Shell. Listen —"

Macklin gathered a loose fistful of Lanneran's shirt and tie. He tightened down. "Rostoff faked that riot. He and some of his Party thugs from New York. Pretending to be Cossacks. Why?"

"Look, Shell —"

Macklin chopped at Lanneran's jaw. "It was a gag to make me sore at Amalgamated. Wasn't it? Talk, you —"

"I'll teach you to slug me!" Lanneran's lifted knee took Macklin in the groin and doubled him over.

Pain screamed through Macklin's belly. He fought it, straightened himself and slammed his knuckles at Lanneran's face.

"A gag to make sure I'd change those specifications. You'd have got me out of the hall ahead of the police if Peggy hadn't done it first. Peggy was right! I was a fool. Maybe you're all taking Moscow orders."

Lanneran's lips peeled back. He didn't have to admit anything: his beady eyes held confession enough. Macklin's sledgehammer fist knocked him into the corridor wall. He bounced and let out a yawp for help.

Help came from the rear room. Rostoff and the three local bigwigs jumped Macklin and flailed him with punches, kicked him down. He felt engulfed in black waves of torture, and stopped trying to defend himself. His strength was gone.

Jack Lanneran panted: "He got wise."

"Too bad." This was Rostoff. "We needed him for that Amalgamated business. Now I guess he'll have to be taken care of. He knows too much. He would be dangerous."

Macklin spoke bitterly, out of a painful fog: "So that's what happened to Obrowski: he was getting out of control. You let him have it in the fake riot. That scheme to ruin the machine tools didn't come from Obrowski. He couldn't typewrite. I should've known."

Macklin's world was upside down. Rostoff the liberator. Rostoff the patriot, the laboring man's friend.

Rostoff the fifth columnist and murderer!

His beliefs shaken and destroyed, Shell Macklin was buffeted by rising tides of wrath. Masquerading as patriotism, the Party had duped him. Had almost brought him to treachery against his flag, as probably many another American had been hoodwinked. The Party wanted America's rearmament program weakened. Why?

Lanneran spoke to Rostoff. "Why liquidate him yet, comrade? We can still make him go through with his job."

Macklin choked. He came to his haunches. "Go ahead and slug me. Knock me off. But by the Eternal, I won't change those specifications."

Lanneran grinned down at him. "This girl you keep talking about. Peggy Ryan. Maybe you'd do it for her if not for the Party."

Macklin realized the import of the threat. It drove sanity out of him. He came off the floor like an explosion. He slammed himself at Lanneran.

Somebody maced him over the skull. His lights went out. He didn't even feel himself falling.

PEGGY RYAN was there when he snapped out of it. She was in an adjoining room, trussed to a chair. They let Macklin look at her through a crack in the doorway.

Lanneran whispered: "It was easy, pal. A phone call did it. Now what do you say?"

Macklin couldn't answer. He was too full of seething helplessness. He'd brought this on himself — and on Peggy. It had been building up ever since he first mentioned her name tonight. Naturally a cagey bunch like Rostoff and Lanneran and the others would be smart enough to take advantage.

Macklin had popped off about his love for Peggy. Now they were using her as a lever. Unless he obeyed orders, something would happen to her.

Probably it would happen even if he did obey orders. Having snatched her, they most likely wouldn't dare turn her loose. Too risky. The same with Macklin. He knew they'd remove him after he had served his purpose. It stood to reason.

He thought of Peggy: soft, feminine, trying to make him see his folly. And failing so utterly that now her life was weighed against the balance of his misguided ideologies. This was what Communism had brought him to!

His agony was more than physical, now. Even if he were free, he couldn't fight this thing single-handed. It was too vast. It had its poisonous roots all over the land. Nothing short of complete disclosure could destroy it; and it would take the government itself to do that. The government Shell Macklin had reviled . . .

But for him it was all over.

Jack Lanneran prodded him ungently with the muzzle of a gun. "Make up your mind, chump." Bluff, hearty Jack Lanneran. The man who'd share his last dime with you. Or his last bullet! "Do we fix those specifications now?"

We. Plural. And the other guy had the gun. Macklin let his shoulders sag. "If I say yes, will you turn Peggy loose? I guess I'll do it — for her. Don't care what happens to me."

"Sure, pal. Sure. Soon as I tell the boys you did the job we turn her loose." A lie, probably, but the only thing he had to bank on.

Macklin pretended to believe. "Let's go," he said.

"That's better, pal." They went out into the night. "Here's my car. You better drive. I got a handful of gun."

Macklin drove. He parked at the Amalgamated plant and took Lanneran past the watchman at the gate: into the tool and die division; into his own cubbyhole of an office, beyond the view of night shift workmen. Lanneran's pocketed automatic cocked, ready to spit death if Macklin hesitated.

The locked desk was where those final specifications were. Macklin keyed the drawer and pulled out the sheaf of papers that represented dozens of machine tools. More than five hundred hours of skilled labor shining in steel for every single sheet and there were dozens of them. All awaiting final touches, last-minute patterning.

One alteration on each specification; one change on each tool. That was all it would take to throw the entire Amalgamated plant into chaos — and into inactivity for another six precious months of national unpreparedness. A big coup for the fifth columnists. A mighty big coup—if they pulled it.

Macklin picked up a fountain pen, got ready to change certain figures on the sheets of paper.

"Need ink," he said. He dipped the pen into a well; thumbed its plunger. His hand was shaking. He steadied it. Now was the time.

Suddenly he swung around, chancing Lanneran's bullet. He aimed the pen squarely at Lanneran's face and squeezed the plunger button. A stream of black ink drove full into Lanneran's eyes.

Lanneran yowled as the stuff blinded him. He let go of his gun and clawed at his eyes.

Macklin doubled both fists and bashed outward with them — twice — driving home the blows so hard that he could feel it all the way up into his own shoulders. So that his whole body ached.

Like a chopped tree, Lanneran fell. His head hit the desk's edge, making a sound too horrible for memory to bear; then he was on the floor. He would never get up again.

Panting, Macklin picked up Lanneran's automatic, turned and grabbed his phone. His shaking fingers slotted into dial holes. Somebody answered: "Party headquarters."

"Rostoff, please." Macklin tried to simulate Lanneran's voice.

A pause. Then: "Who's this?"

"Lanneran. Hurry — get Rostoff."

The other voice was edged with suspicion. "You don't sound like Lanneran for my money. Where are you?"

Macklin broke out in cold sweat. He talked fast. "Amalgamated. I'm nervous. You know why. Comrade, for Heaven's sake get Rostoff."

A grunt, then another pause. And finally Rostoff s voice. Macklin breathed deeply, feeling weak.

"The job's done, Comrade Rostoff. I'm bringing Macklin downtown again.

"Good. Do that."

Macklin rang off. He thumbed the greasy phone book, hunting a number. The only number that could help him now. The F.B.I.

FUNNY how a guy's ideas can change. Today, Shell Macklin had considered the F.B.I. in the same light he thought of a Gestapo or an

Ogpu. Agency of a government that needed to be overthrown and destroyed. Bunch of snooping spies working for Capital.

Now he knew better. Capital and Labor — they both stood for the American way. Destroy one and you maroon the other. Then you get dictatorship: the rule of force, the rule of murder.

Macklin found his number and called it.

His words spilled into the mouthpiece: gasping, blurted, incoherent. But he got his meaning across. They understood.

He hurled the phone from him and pelted for the exit. There was Lanneran's car. He slid under the wheel, tortured the starter with his foot. He moved.

Stop lights? Traffic? Shell Macklin broke all the rules there were. Cops? Let them follow. He wanted them to follow. But as usual, there weren't any cops when you needed them most.

Just as well, maybe. Siren-sound might warn Rostoff and the others. Better arrive quietly. Better let gunfire make the necessary noise when the time came.

Here was headquarters. Macklin locked his brakes, piled out, slammed himself into the building. Gaining the rear room, he smashed the door off its hinges. "Now, you rats!"

They were all there. Including Rostoff. And including Peggy Ryan, tied to a chair at the far end of the room. She cried out when she saw Macklin.

He faced the men who were his enemies. His, and his country's. "Stay still!"

One of them took a chance: pulled a .38 and cut loose. Macklin felt the sting of a soft-nosed hornet through his thigh. He went listing sidewise as his leg kicked out from under him.

That saved his life; saved him from a second slug that would have taken him between the eyes. Instead, it chewed plaster from the wall behind him. There wasn't a third, because Macklin's own trigger was pumping.

He splashed bullets like water from a hose. He sprayed the room. He hurled lead until he had no more lead to hurl. Until there were no more men before him —

Except Rostoff.

Rostoff said: "You're through, Macklin. You're out of bullets."

Macklin hit him with the empty gun. Hit him in the mouth, as he himself had been struck by Rostoff s blackjack earlier that night.

The bald man spat teeth and blood. He kept boring in. He was inhuman. You slugged him over the hairless skull and he refused to fall. He kept coming at you no matter what you did.

You couldn't escape him. He was a fiend. His fingers were steel.

They were steel bands around Macklin's gullet. It was mad. It was monstrous, like a nightmare. It was something out of Hell itself, this thing that was happening.

Macklin's lungs were afire. His neck was a constricted agony. Black blur swam in his eyes. The stink of Rostoff s breath was in his nostrils. The fear of death entered his heart and grew there like a poisonous mushroom.

Yet he had every reason to live now; he had to live.

He struggled. He tried savagely to fight off this monster and all he represented. He bludgeoned that slippery skull one last desperate time.

Rostoff s hold weakened. Now he had to go down. You can't stay on your feet when your head's been hammered open.

But Rostoff did. He remained upright. He came back at Macklin with murder in his eyes; and as Shell waited for that charge, Peggy screamed.

Macklin knew he was washed up. This time Rostoff would finish him. He braced himself.

Peggy screamed again, "Shell — Shell —"

Her eyes were on the smashed door. Men were boiling into the room. G-men with guns. They nailed Rostoff to the wall.

Shell Macklin pitched forward on his face.

Hospital-smell awakened him: clean, pungent. He was on a white bed in a white room. Peggy was leaning over him. "Shell . . . darling!"

"Hello, Peg." He grinned weakly. He had things to tell her; things he was ashamed of. What a blind fool he'd been, for instance. How close he'd come to being a Benedict Arnold. He tried to find the words. It was tough.

But he was saved from that.

She put her soft hand on his cheek; it was cool and soothing. "There's only one thing I want to hear you say now, Shell."

So he said it. "I love you," he whispered. Then he slept again. He was content. He had earned enough glory.

THE COCK CROWS "MURDER"

SHERIFF JIM VONNER had little stomach for the job confronting him, but he had to see it through. A quarter of a mile distant from Sash Townsend's Farm, he doused his headlamps and shut off his ignition. Coasting the rest of the way through darkness, he signaled the two following cars, laden with temporary deputies, to do likewise.

The excited noises issuing from the big gray Townsend barn effectively covered the lesser sounds of the three-car motorcade's arrival in the farmyard. Sheriff Jim braked to a stop and turned to Brod Townsend, the sullen and glowering man beside him.

"You still want to go on with this, Brod?"

"I'm certain." Brod's voice was unpleasantly nasal. "Otherwise, why do you think I swore out the complaint?"

"But Sash is your brother."

"He's a lawbreaker!"

In the gloom, Brod's lips seemed a thin, horny slit, like the mouth of a snapping-turtle.

The sheriff sighed heavily from the depths of his vast girth. There was scarcely a man in the county he couldn't call friend, and beyond doubt the yelling crowd in Sash Townsend's barn would include plenty of Jim Vonner's pinochle cronies and fishing companions.

It was one thing to apprehend thieves and murderers, but to arrest his intimates merely because they patronized a sport frowned upon by the statutes was something else again. Even more personal was Sheriff Jim's reluctance to take the younger Townsend brother into custody.

"I don't like it, Brod," he said. "Strikes me you're packing a grudge because Evelyn got engaged to Sash instead of you."

"Let's leave Evelyn's name out of it. You're the sheriff, even if you are her father. There wasn't anything in your oath of office that said you couldn't arrest your future son-in-law, far as I can remember." Chuckling maliciously, Brod peered into the tonneau at Ed Fabring, local justice of the peace. "Hope you brought your law book along, Ed."

Fabring was shrunken and wizened, with a face like a dried windfall apple, liver-blotched and wrinkled.

"I'm ready to set up court and assess fines right in the barn," he answered.

"Fines, hell! Jail terms is what they deserve."

"You wouldn't tell me my business, would you, Brod?" the J.P. inquired tartly.

Brod muttered a surly apology. Sheriff Jim, hearing it, smiled to himself. It wasn't often that Brod Townsend apologized to anybody, but this time he was dealing with a man who held the mortgage on his acres. That made quite a difference.

From the two other cars, seven deputies, indiscriminately rounded up and sworn in at the village, piled out. Jim Vonner unwedged his corpulence from behind his steering wheel and led his forces into the lantern-lighted barn.

His sortie possessed the virtue of complete surprise. Of the twenty-five or thirty yelling men grouped about the improvised cockpit, not a single one noticed the sheriff's advent. Their concerted attention was riveted upon the battle taking place in the center of the circular space where two gamecocks, one a ruby-eyed Carolina Blue and the other a symmetrically streamlined Whitehackle, were locked in death-combat.

Their natural spurs augmented by attached steel gaffs, like tapered needles, the cocks shuffled each other in a blur of bloody motion. Suddenly, faster than the eye could follow, the Whitehackle shifted, fluttered high into the air and came down with his gaffs flashing in the yellow light. Sharp metal penetrated the Carolina Blue's brain, and the fight was finished. The Blue squawked once and subsided into a quivering heap of ruffled feathers. The Whitehackle crowed raucous triumph over his kill.

"Sorry, boys," Sheriff Jim said, "but you're all under arrest."

Pit-fowl handlers, referee and startled audience went abruptly silent. They were too surprised for confusion, as every eye turned toward Jim Vonner and his intruders. The sheriff made a wry grimace of discomfort under this hostile scrutiny. From somewhere in the crowd, an angry voice said:

"How come, Jim? This ain't like you!"

It was Harley Eblen who spoke, Harley Eblen, the sheriff's partner on many a fishing and hunting expedition. He was big and blond and ordinarily easygoing. But truculent now, his blue eyes blazed with unconcealed ire.

Sheriff Jim shrugged his fat shoulders.

"Don't blame me, Harley. Cocking mains are against the law. Squire Fabring, here, made out the warrant."

"Fabring, eh?" Eblen took a threatening step toward the little J.P. "Why, you runty, sawed-off . . ."

Sheriff Jim interposed his bulk.

"No need to get hotheaded, Harley. It won't do any good." He looked around. "Where's Sash Townsend?"

"He went out to get . . ." somebody started so say, but another voice, anonymous within the crowd, shouted a warning.

"Shut up! Don't tell 'em anything!" And Harley Eblen, taking this up, grinned sourly. "Sash ain't been here at all," he interjected. "He don't know anything about our little party."

That was a lie, of course. They were covering up for Sash, since he would be the most culpable of the group, having supplied his barn as a place for the cocking main. Sheriff Jim's full lips twitched in appreciation of this quick loyalty. No matter what else happened now, Sash was out of it. And a man hates to be put to the embarrassment of arresting his own daughter's future husband.

Ed Fabring cleared his throat. "Reckon I might as well open court here and now. Somebody get me a box or something for a desk."

"I will," Harley Eblen volunteered, somewhat surprisingly. There was a partitioned-off room at the back of the barn, and Harley opened the rough door and stepped into the gloom beyond. Chicken sounds filtered from behind the board paneling, then there was a silence that lasted too long.

"Maybe he skipped," Brod Townsend muttered nasally. "It'd be just like him."

"Skipped?" Ed Fabring said. "He'd better not! I'll fine him for contempt!"

He scuttled to the door and went into the rear room. Squawkings and wing-flutterings sounded again, and Fabring's voice yowled:

"Here, now! Stop that! Damnation! You, Harry Eblen, where are you?" Overturned lumber clattered.

"Trouble in there!" Brod Townsend grunted. He leaped to the door, and shadows swallowed him. Suddenly he was shouting: "Everybody come in here quick! Bring a light! My God —"

Sheriff Jim hoisted his poundage onto a bench, reached for a dangling kerosene lantern and wrenched it down. Moving deceptively fast for all his overweight, he gained the rear room and plunged in.

He almost stumbled over Ed Fabring, writhing on the floor. Blood was spurting from the little J.P.'s wizened throat, where jugular vein and carotid artery had been slashed open. He was still alive, but no power on earth could keep him that way, Jim Vonner ruefully realized. Blinking, twisting, clawing spasmodically at his gashed gullet, Fabring seemed to be trying to say something, but the words wouldn't come.

Vonner felt a little sick. He looked for Harley Eblen but couldn't see him. An open doorway gave access to the outer darkness, mute testimony to Eblen's flight from the barn. Far back in a corner of the room, beyond the strength of the light, Brod Townsend was scrambling around among flimsy wooden crates containing penned gamecocks, cursing them bitterly.

At last he came forward, his lacerated hands clenched about a profanely squawking Shawlneck fighter.

"Look!" he panted, holding the fowl aloft before the men who crowded and milled into the room.

On the floor, Ed Fabring stiffened convulsively, a wet rattling noise in his throat, then the breath reluctantly oozed out of him in a final gurgling suspiration and he was still.

"Dead," Sheriff Jim announced morosely. He looked up at Brod Townsend. "What's that you've got?"

"A man-killer!" Brod answered. "Caught him over behind the crates. Don't know how he got loose, but . . ."

The sheriff's nostrils fluttered as he drew a deep breath. "Man-killer?" he said. "Mean to say that rooster cut Ed Fabring's throat?"

"Must have. That was what we heard when Ed started yelling. Look at these spurs."

The Shawlneck was heeled with twin slasher gaffs, each blade at least two-and-a-half inches long. Flat and murderously honed to the sharpness of surgical scalpels, the bright steel was still sticky with blood. Somebody whispered audibly.

"That's one of Sash's birds! Meanest cock in the county, too. Soon fly at you as look at you. Reminds me of a case I read about, down in Florida. Shawlneck cock killed his handler, clean as a whistle!"

Sheriff Jim was silent a moment, digesting this, adding it to what he knew. First, he considered Sash Townsend's absence, then Harley Eblen's flight, then the death of Ed Fabring at the spurs of a cock belonging to Sash. The picture wasn't a pretty one, and parts of it seemed somehow out of focus.

Very cautiously, while Brod held the fowl, Sheriff Jim untied the wax cords that held the slasher gaffs in place. He wrapped the red-stained blades in a handkerchief and thrust them into the pocket of his short jacket.

"Pen that chicken up, Brod," he ordered. "The rest of you boys can go on home. There won't be any fines laid tonight"

"Can we take our gamecocks?"

"I guess so."

"And you ain't arrestin' us, after all?"

"Not for chicken fighting when I've got a murder on my hands," the sheriff answered slowly.

"Murder!" Brod Townsend's voice twanged shrilly upward. "How can you call it murder? You're not accusing Sash of gaffing that rooster and turning him loose to kill, are you? That's crazy. How could Sash know Squire Fabring'd be the one who'd come in here and get it?"

Jim Vonner wagged his head from side to side, heavily, in negation. It was funny, he thought, how blood always turned out to be thicker than water when the time came. Brod had been anxious enough to see his brother arrested for running an illegal cocking main, but when it came down to a murder charge he was swift to leap to Sash's defense.

"I didn't accuse Sash," the sheriff answered evenly. "Speaking of him, though, I think we'd better see if we can find him."

He turned to a deputy. "You run down to the village and make arrangements for Doc Blayne and the undertaker to come out here right away. The rest of you boys better leave, too."

Slowly, one by unwilling one, the gathering melted off. Sheriff Jim found a blanket in one of the horse stalls and used it to cover Ed Fabring's corpse. Then, with Brod Townsend at his heels, he left the barn and went over to the neat little farmhouse by the road.

There were no lights in any of the windows. The sheriff knocked on the door, eliciting no response.

"Sash! Sash Townsend! Come out here!" he called.

Again there was no answer.

He tried the door and found it unlocked, but a search of the house revealed no trace of Sash Townsend.

"Queer," Sheriff Jim mused. "He ought to be somewhere around. Unless those boys were telling the truth that Sash didn't know anything about the main here tonight."

"It might be," Brod said.

"And yet somebody tied those slashers on that Shawlneck and turned him loose in the little room."

"How about Harley Eblen?" Brod muttered. "He went in to get a box for a desk, remember. And then he ran away."

"We'll go see Harley," the sheriff agreed. "Maybe we'll find him home."

They did find Harley Eblen home, over near the next section line. He greeted his visitors warily.

"If you're thinking you can confiscate my gamecocks . . ."

"I figured that's what happened," Sheriff Jim smiled. "You had some valuable roosters crate-penned in the back room of Sash's barn and you didn't want 'em taken away from you, so you grabbed the first handy excuse to go in there and save 'em. You carried the crates out the back door while we thought you were looking for a box, loaded em on your wagon and drove on home."

"Maybe so, maybe not. Anyhow, you can't prove I had any cocks in that barn. Not now you can't."

THE sheriff pursed his lips. "I'm not trying to prove anything like that, Harley. I got more important matters on my mind. I'm looking for the man responsible for Ed Fabring's death."

"Fabring's death!"

"No use pretending you don't know about it!" Brod Townsend said bitterly. "You tried to take a poke at the squire when we first busted in on your party. You were sore at him. You could have tied those spurs on that rooster and turned him loose, knowing Ed would come in looking for you."

Harley Eblen blinked his bewilderment.

"What rooster you talking about? I don't get it."

Sheriff Jim explained tersely.

"A Shawlneck cut Ed's throat with slasher gaffs, Harley. Know any-thing about it?"

Eblen wasn't angry, now. He was disturbed.

"Slashers? No, I don't know a thing. You got to believe me, Jim!"

"Well, then, what about Sash Townsend? Can you tell me where he went?"

"You mean Sash is missin'!"

"I can't seem to find him."

"But — but he just went out to the house to get some beer for the boys, a little before you showed up."

"So he was taking part in the main."

Eblen reddened. "Guess I shouldn't have said that. But hell, Jim,

Sash wouldn't have no reason to want to kill Ed Fabring! Besides, maybe the whole thing was an accident. That cock might have got loose some way, and . . ."

"You might be right," the sheriff sighed. "I don't know. But there don't seem much more I can do about it until I find Sash and ask him. Come along, Brod. I'll drive you home."

Later, alone, Jim Vonner returned to Sash Townsend's place and saw that Fabring's body had been removed to the village mortuary. Nobody had seen Sash Townsend. He seemed to have vanished into thin air. Going home, the sheriff pondered this, trying to establish a reason for Sash having run away. The more he thought about it, the more it seemed that there could be only one plausible answer. And the answer troubled him, largely because he was in no position to prove it.

He found Evelyn, his daughter waiting up for him when he reached his house. She seemed distraught, and her eyes were reddened as if she might recently have been crying.

"Something wrong, honey?" he asked gently.

Lips tremulous, fingers plucking nervously at her dress, she turned around and faced him.

"What happened at Sash's place? Why should he have to run away and hide?"

"So he's been here," Sheriff Jim said, his inflection a statement of fact rather than a query.

Evelyn sucked in her breath, swiftly.

"I didn't say he'd been here."

"You didn't have to, honey. But how else would you have known anything happened out to his farm unless he came here and told you? How else would you know he'd run away?"

"Th-that still doesn't answer my question, Daddy. I want to know what trouble Sash is in. Please tell me."

Her moist eyes implored him as well as her voice.

He debated his reply, realizing finally that sooner or later she'd learn the truth anyhow.

"There was a murder," he said. "Squire Fabring was killed."

"And — and you think Sash did it? Oh-h-h, Daddy!"

HE took her into his arms, soothingly, and his own heart was disturbed. He knew how much the girl thought of Sash Townsend, knew how poignant her grief must be at the idea of her sweetheart being involved in a killing. But somehow, when he tried to give tongue to some comforting word, he found himself inarticulate.

"There, there, honey. Don't cry. You mustn't cry," was all he could say. She pushed herself free of him.

"I'm going to Sash. He needs me!" she cried.

"I wish you wouldn't, Evelyn. It's late. And maybe I need you, too."

"You!" Her lips curled bitterly. "You think Sash is a murderer — just like all the others do."

Her scorn hurt him, her contempt stung him to the quick. His mouth twisted in a wry smile.

"I wish you'd trust me, honey. I want you to be happy. You know that," he murmured.

"Then clear Sash of this horrible charge! Prove you want me to be happy!"

"I'll try. It may take time, though. You see, baby, there are certain things I'm not sure of, yet. A lot depends on Sash himself. You wouldn't be willing to take me to him, would you?"

"So that you can arrest him? No!"

"Then promise me one thing. Promise me you won't see him yourself until I say it's all right."

She stared at him, dubiously.

"Why do you ask me that?"

"I can't explain, honey. I'm just asking you to trust me."

At last, his daughter smiled wanly.

"All right, Daddy. I'll do what you ask."

"Thanks, baby." He patted her cheek. "Now run along to bed. It's late."

Long after she had gone upstairs, he remained in the living room, pacing the floor, examining those slasher gaffs that had brought death to Ed Fabring. It was dawn before he finally took a nap on the couch, a nap roiled by unpleasant dreams. The fragrant redolence of coffee awakened him, and he saw that it was morning. Evelyn was in the kitchen, preparing breakfast. She seemed less fearful, less upset, now that daylight had come.

The meal finished, Sheriff Jim arose to answer the ringing of the telephone. It was Doc Blayne, down in the village, informing him that the coroner's inquest over Ed Fabring's body would be held that afternoon.

"I'll be on hand," the sheriff said gravely. "And I'll have some things to say."

When the time came, though, he found difficulty in wording his testimony before the jury. For one thing, every other witness — and they included the men who had attended the cocking main at Sash Townsend's barn as well as the special deputies Sheriff Jim had taken with him on the raid — stoutly maintained that Fabring's death must have been an accident. Harley Eblen was loudest in this assertion, which was natural enough when one considered how Harley might have had an opportunity to attach those gaffs to the Shawlneck's spurs.

"The way I see it," Harley said from the witness chair, "that cock was bein' readied for a match, and somehow or other he got loose. Then, when the squire went into that room, the bird flew at him. Shawlnecks are vicious that way. It's happened before."

Lumbering ponderously to the stand and being sworn, the sheriff contradicted all that had been said.

"We're dealing with a plain case of murder, and that's the only verdict should be brought in. Murder at the hands of a person or persons unknown."

Doc Blayne peered at him over the tops of hornrimmed spectacles.

"Mind telling us how you arrive at that conclusion, Jim?"

"I'd sooner not, but I will if you make me."

"I think I'd better insist, Jim."

The sheriff looked out over the faces that thronged the little hearing room, witnesses and the merely curious who packed the place from wall to wall.

"There was an eyewitness," he said at last.

"Eyewitness to what? To the tying of those gaffs on the Shawlneck?"

"Something like that."

"Who saw it?"

"Sash Townsend."

"How do you know that, Jim?"

"Sash was at my place last night. He talked with my girl."

"You mean he told her he saw . . ."

"No," Sheriff Jim interrupted quickly. "He didn't tell her what he saw. But he'll tell me when I find him."

"You know where to look for him?"

"I think Evelyn knows where he is. She'll lead me to him when the time comes. Maybe tonight."

The coroner excused Jim Vonner, then, and he drove his car home. At once he started packing a bag, unostentatiously slipping a revolver into it before Evelyn saw what he was doing. It was dusk when he came downstairs, carrying the suitcase.

His daughter widened her eyes.

"You're going somewhere, Daddy?"

"For a day or two. Business. I won't have time for supper, honey. Sorry." He hesitated.

"About that promise you made me," he added.

"You mean — about seeing Sash?"

He nodded. "You can take it back, now. Something tells me this trip I'm making will clear him. You might tell him so if you want to."

"Oh, Daddy!"

Her arms went around his thick neck, gratefully. Her lips sweetly brushed his cheek.

He went out to the car, then, and drove away. But he journeyed only as far as Harley Eblen's farm, reaching it with the coming of darkness.

"Got a job for you, Harley," he said to the big, yellow-haired man.

"What is it, Jim?"

"Can't tell you. Just come along." The sheriff opened his bag and took out his revolver, jamming it into his pocket as Harley Eblen's eyes widened. Then the two men set forth across Harley's plowed fields, heading back in the direction of Sheriff Jim's house.

It was a thirty minute walk. Nearing there, the sheriff pointed to a bobbing lantern yellowly pinpointing the darkness ahead as someone set out from the house, moving toward the bottom lands along Carp Creek.

"Evelyn," Sheriff Jim whispered succinctly. "Hurry. Don't let her know she's being followed."

At a tangent whose angle would intersect with the girl's course, Jim Vonner and Harley Eblen stole forward. The sheriff felt sure of himself now, and his heart pounded with a curious admixture of sensations — incipient triumph tinged with something he realized was fear. He cast a narrow glance at the man beside him.

"You got a gun, Harley?"

"No."

"Here's hoping you won't need one. Come on, now. Remember that old spring house down by the creek? Sort of set against the bank, partly a cave, like?"

"Yes."

"That's the place. Hurry. But no noise."

Their feet silent in the soft, rich loam, they reached the stream bank just as Evelyn, swinging her lantern, neared the abandoned spring house. Her voice called softly through the night, velvet against velvet.

"Sash. Sash, darling."

A man came out of the spring house. At the same moment, a shadow stirred in the alders to Sheriff Jim's left. The sheriff saw the glint of metal, launched his bulk at the shadow and the metallic glint just as a gun bellowed spiteful flame.

It was like a sledgehammer blow hitting him in the ribs, pounding the breath out of his lungs, searing his flesh like the sting of a red-hot hornet. But the bullet couldn't stop him. He smashed into his quarry before a second shot could be fired.

"Got you, Brod Townsend!" he panted. "I figured you'd follow my girl here and try to kill your brother because he knew too much. That's why I said as much as I did, back at the inquest. You were there, and you got scared. Looks like my trap worked."

White, snarling, helpless under the sheriff's smothering weight, Brod Townsend squalled nasal curses.

"Let me up! I'll kill the lot of you! Damn you!"

"You're through killing," Sheriff Jim said.

He cast a quick glance at his daughter in Sash Townsend's arms, over by the spring house, and at Harley Eblen standing nearby, open-mouthed with wonderment.

"You can't prove I killed Ed Fabring!" Brod wheeled.

"That's almost a confession in itself, Brod. Not that I need it, now. By trying to shoot Sash, you've given your game away. Almost from the start, I figured you were the murderer, but I couldn't prove it without some kind of a showdown. This is it."

"You're crazy!"

"Not quite, Brod. You see, I happen to know Squire Fabring had a mortgage on your farm and was going to foreclose. That gave you a motive for murdering him. Once he was dead, his estate would be tied up in court for quite a time. Long enough to give you a chance to get some money together, maybe, and satisfy the mortgage."

"That's a lie!"

Undisturbed, the sheriff rumbled on.

"You brought that charge against Sash and forced me to raid his cocking main, knowing Fabring would go along. You figured you'd get a chance to kill him some time or other during the commotion, and you had your murder method all planned. You had a pair of slasher gaffs, and you intended to sneak up behind him and cut his throat on both sides, holding the gaffs in your hands.

"Then you'd tie the gaffs to a gamecock and claim the whole thing was accidental. It worked out just that way, too."

"I never . . ."

"But you went wrong because you didn't know much about cock-fighting, Brod. It so happens that in the United States, slasher gaffs are never used. Americans heel their birds with steel spurs, round from socket to point, like needles. Slashers are sort of like little knives, and the only places you find 'em are in Mexico and Cuba and South America.

"You must have sent to Mexico for your pair, most likely. We can check that later. Main thing is, I smelled a rat as soon as I saw those slashers on the Shawlneck. In fact, using a pair of 'em was another bad mistake you made.

"Slashers are never used in pairs. A gamecock'd cut his own legs off if he was heeled with two of the things. They just tie one onto his left spur when they're used at all. I been around enough mains to know that much."

Brod Townsend's eyes began to hold fear. He mumbled something nobody could understand.

"Seeing these things," Sheriff Jim went on, "I knew just how you killed Fabring. You followed him into the little room, took him from behind, and then went over into a dark corner and tied the gaffs to that Shawlneck while yelling for the rest of us to come in. But I couldn't prove it."

"You still can't." Brod Townsend sneered at the sheriff.

"Wrong, Brod. When Sash ran away, I knew he had a good reason. What was that reason, I asked myself? And the answer was plain. He must've looked into that back room, through the doorway, just as you were cutting Fabring's throat with your slashers. Sash is your brother, and he'd sooner leave the county than testify you into the noose, I reckon. That way, he's a lot different from you.

"I'll admit you pretended to come to his defense when I hinted he might be the guilty one, but that was just to cover your own tracks. When the time came, and you thought Sash had the goods on you, you came here to shut his mouth with a bullet, just as I thought you would."

Sheriff Jim looked up at the younger Townsend. "Now that you see what Brod would've done to you, I reckon you won't hesitate to tell what you saw, eh, Sash?"

Sash didn't have to answer.

"To Hell with all of you!" Brod said. "I'll take a plea and maybe they'll let me off with life."

"Good idea," Sheriff Jim Vonner said, his voice queerly weak.

His wounded side was hurting him, now that the first shock had worn off. He was bleeding pretty badly, too. He could feel it. He beckoned to Harley Eblen.

"Better take over from here on out, Harley," he said.

Then he smiled at his daughter and Sash Townsend. They made a nice-looking couple, all right. He hoped he'd get out of the hospital in time to attend the wedding.

KNIFE IN THE DARK

CHAPTER I

Dead Passenger

THE PILOT knew his trade. I scarcely felt the big airliner's wheels touch the ground. There was no shock, no bounce, no sense of transition from airborne to earthbound. The night was as dark as a pocket in perdition and the storm that had threatened us all the way south from San Francisco was a steady drench now that we had landed in L.A. But at least we had landed, rain or no rain, and presently I would be finding out why the agency had sent me down here in such a hurry to see ex-Senator Cartwain's nephew.

I waited until the plane had made its taxi run to the passenger apron. Then, as soon as they had rolled the portable steps into place and opened the door, I checked out past the stewardess and made my break for the canopied runway to the depot building. Even with my hat brim turned down and my topcoat collar up, I got thoroughly soaked before I reached shelter.

Southern California never does anything by halves. Rain in Los Angeles isn't just rain; it's a feature production. The movie influence, probably.

In the station, a loud-speaker cleared its metallic throat and began telling the arriving travelers where to wait for their luggage. I had none to wait for. The only clothes I had with me were the wet ones I was wearing, so I wasn't interested in baggage announcements. I came alert, though, when I heard my name crackling out of the horn.

"Passenger Palmer just in from San Francisco on Flight Eleven. Passenger Palmer just in from San Francisco on Flight Eleven. Attention Passenger Palmer. Will you please call at the Coastal Airways ticket desk on the east side of the rotunda? Thank you."

When you've been a private detective as long as I have, watchfulness and caution become second nature. I headed for the rotunda's west side, away from where I was wanted, then carefully circled the waiting room. I loitered along casually, as if waiting for an outbound flight.

Passing the newsstand, I dropped a nickel and took a late edition of the *Herald-Express*, held it up before me and pretended to scan the headlines. Under its cover I delved beneath my left armpit, unholstered my stubby .32 automatic, unobtrusively transferred it to the right side pocket of my topcoat and kept my hand on it.

Then I peered over the newspaper toward Coastal's ticket desk.

A TALL, thin man in chauffeur's livery stood there talking to the clerk. In turn, the clerk picked up a phone and spoke into it. Right after that, the loudspeaker repeated its plea. "Would passenger Palmer, just arrived from San Francisco on Flight Eleven, contact Coastal Airways at once? Thank you." Click.

So it was the chauffeur who was having me paged. I decided he looked harmless and I relaxed, moved forward. Then he turned, so that I could see his face, and suddenly there was no more relaxation in me. Tension took its place, a taut, twanging premonition of danger.

I knew the man. Nixon was his name, Edgar Nixon, and he hated my insides. A year ago he had threatened to kill me.

He hadn't been a chauffeur in those days. He had been an obscure lawyer representing an equipment manufacturer under Congressional investigation for war contract irregularities. And I had been the special agent for the Cartwain Committee who had dug up most of the evidence that finally got Nixon's client indicted. It was my last G-job in Washington before I quit and came back to private work out here on the West Coast.

As an unexpected afterpiece to this war contract probe, Nixon himself had been disbarred, fined, and jailed for alleged subornation of perjury. That was a charge with which I'd had nothing to do, and of which I didn't particularly approve. Somehow it seemed to me that he had been made a scapegoat, a whipping boy, merely because he had dared to defend a profiteer. While he might have been misguided in accepting such a tawdry case, I had considered him guilty of nothing worse than unwise judgment.

The Cartwain Committee and the courts, however, thought otherwise. And when Nixon was sentenced he had blamed me for it, had shouted that he would shoot me dead as soon as he was free.

So now he was free.

I waited until his back was to me. Then I walked up behind him, let him feel the prod of the gun in my pocket.

"Looking for me, Nixon?"

Red came up his neck, spread to his ears. "My name isn't Nixon," he said, without turning. A twitching muscle made his shoulder jump under the formfitting brown whipcord tunic.

"But mine is Palmer," I said. "Don Palmer, from San Francisco. Just in on Flight Eleven."

Slowly, then, he faced me. He was having trouble with his breathing, and his muddy eyes were protuberant.

"So you're the Palmer I was to meet!" he choked.

I let that ride. I also let him see it was a gun I had in my pocket.

"You're caught off base, Nixon. Don't try anything you'll regret."

"I — I don't — I wasn't — I didn't intend —"

The airline ticket clerk was looking at us with too much speculation. I walked Nixon across the rotunda to a spot where we had more privacy.

"When did you get out?" I asked.

"Out —?"

"Of prison. Don't spar with me."

"Two — months ago."

"Escape?"

"Parole," he said quickly. "I can prove that. I have papers. I can show you."

"Later," I said. "Right now I'm more interested in why you were having me paged."

"I told you. I was sent to meet a Mr. Palmer coming in on the plane from up north."

"Who sent you?"

"The people I work for. Listen," he added desperately. "They don't know I'm Edgar Nixon. They don't know I'm a jailbird." Droplets of sweat popped out on his forehead. "I took this job under an alias, and — and —"

I studied him, beginning to understand the crazy implausibility of the situation. My agency had despatched me south to see the nephew of former Senator Marcus Cartwain. Therefore, if Nixon had been sent to pick me up, there was only one possible conclusion I could draw.

"Do you mean to say you're chauffeuring for the Cartwains?" I demanded. "Ex-Senator Cartwain, who headed the Cartwain Committee that wrecked you?"

"Y-yes." He spread his hands. "Give me a break, Palmer! Don't tell them who I am. If you do, they'll fire me. All I want is a chance."

"Once you threatened to kill me," I interrupted him. "Now you beg me for favors."

"I didn't m-mean those threats." The nervous tic twitched his shoulder again. "It was just that I saw my reputation, my career, my whole life going down in ruins. I blamed you, then. But later I realized you had nothing to do with it."

"Nice of you."

"It was my own fault, for trying to defend that profiteer. By tying up with a fellow like that I left myself wide open for trouble. Marcus Cartwain was running for reelection and he made political capital out of smearing me. Not that it did his campaign any good when it came to count the votes."

"So all right," I said. "So he was licked, and he left his home state and retired to California. So now you're one of his servants, and that makes no sense whatever. He must realize you hate him for what he did to you. Then why would he hire you, alias or no alias? Don't tell me he didn't recognize you. I did. You haven't changed that much in a year."

"He hasn't recognized me," Nixon said, "because he's blind."

I felt my own eyes widening. "What?"

"It's true. He lost his sight a few months ago. He hasn't let the newspapers know it. Pride, I guess. But I found it out, and I applied for the job when his former chauffeur quit, and — well, he hired me."

"Why?"

"Why did he hire me? I'm a good driver. Maybe a better driver than I was lawyer. More careful, anyway."

"No. Why did you go after the job? What's your game? Revenge? Waiting for a chance to get even?"

"I'd be silly to admit that, even if it were true. You'd warn Cartwain. You'd tell him who I am."

"I would indeed."

"But it's not true. Maybe I had some such idea at first. I've had some pretty bitter moments. But not any more. I'm playing it straight, and if you'll just give me a break I'll keep on playing it straight. I give you my oath."

The oath of a paroled convict isn't often a thing of too great substance. Yet somehow, as I looked at Nixon, I felt that he meant what he said. He seemed sincere, and as a rule I'm not easily fooled.

I gripped his forearm, squeezed it hard for emphasis.

"I make no promises," I said. "I want time to think it over. But for the time being, I won't give you away — and never mind the gratitude."

Then I said: "Now tell me why the Cartwains wanted me sent down to see them."

"That I wouldn't know. Young Gerry — I mean Mr. Gerald — is waiting for you out in the car. The Senator's nephew, you know." Nixon's lips curved downward at the corners. "He didn't like getting wet, so he sent me in after you."

"Let's go," I said, and made for the exit.

The rain was still a production number. I was dripping when I reached the limousine; so was Nixon.

He opened the tonneau door for me.

"Mr. Gerald, sir, this is Don Palmer of San Francisco."

Inside the car, Gerald sat in the far corner — dapper, expensively tailored, his expression a little sardonic. Faint lines of dissipation were beginning to etch themselves into his face, and even without the dome light I could see he needed some sun-tan to relieve his unhealthy pallor.

Behind the chauffeur's back, I put a quick finger to my lips. Whatever young Cartwain had to tell me, I didn't want it discussed where Nixon could overhear. That seemed only a reasonable precaution under the circumstances.

Poker-faced, Gerald neither greeted me nor acknowledged my impulsive gesture. That was all right, though. It indicated that he had caught the signal and knew how to obey orders. I was pleased by this, because it helped modify the original impression of him that I'd had back in Washington a year before.

Then he had struck me as a hard-drinking, hard-spending playboy with more money than brains. Now, I reflected, he was beginning to show signs of sense. He was growing up.

I got in beside him, sitting in the opposite corner so my wet topcoat wouldn't soak his suit the way the coat was soaking the mohair upholstery. Up front, Nixon slid under his wheel, got his engine and twin windshield wipers going. The long, luxurious car whispered into forward motion.

I whispered, too, after first making sure the glass partition was closed between tonneau and front compartment.

"Easy with the conversation until later. That is, if what you want to tell me is confidential."

Gerald nodded absently. The limousine cleared an uneven place in the paving, then flowed like poured oil through Burbank and out toward the Valley. Our tires hissed steadily against the rain-slick asphalt and the side windows began to steam up, so that the occasional service station neon signs we passed glowed like ghostfire, vague and intangible.

Then we made an abrupt turn — and young Cartwain toppled out of his corner to sag limply against me, like a rag doll.

Startled, I shoved him off.

"What's the matter with you?" I said sharply. "Are you drunk?"

He didn't answer.

I propped him by pressing my hand against his side. Something wet and sticky met my fingers, something that might be blood. It was blood, from a stab wound. I touched his neck, found no pulsation where the artery ran.

Gerald Cartwain was dead. I had been riding with a corpse.

CHAPTER II

Disappearing Corpse

IN RAPID sequence, I reviewed everything I could remember since getting into the car. I recalled the way young Cartwain had sat in his corner, unmoving, not speaking. I had thought his silence was because of the warning signal I had given him, but now I knew better. I knew he had never seen that signal. And his faintly supercilious smile, I realized, had been something else entirely — the beginning of risus sardonicus, the death grin.

Nor had his pallor been from dissipation. He had lost color as his blood drained out of that knife wound in his side. Even his head nodding could be logically explained. That had happened when the limousine had jounced on a rough place in the paving.

In brief, he had been dead from the start. He had been murdered before I climbed in beside him.

I wedged him back in his corner of the seat, then got out the automatic from my topcoat pocket. Leaning forward, I slid the glass partition open behind Edgar Nixon's head. Then I pressed my gun muzzle to the nape of his neck.

"Pull over," I said.

He winced at the feel of steel on him. Maybe the tone of my voice had something to do with it, too.

"Wh-what —"

"Pull over and stop."

"But — but —"

"You heard me, killer. I'm not fooling."

He slapped down hard on his brake pedal and the limousine edged over to the right, sliding a little on the wet street. The sudden deceleration sent Gerald Cartwain's body lurching frontward. His dead face hit the partition with a sickening sound. Then, grotesquely, he landed in a crumpled heap on the floor.

The car stopped.

I opened the left-hand door and stepped out fast, so that the merest shifting of my gun kept its sights lined on Nixon. At the moment, there was no traffic in either direction. There was only the incessant rain and the sound of its steady drumming.

We were in an undeveloped section of the Valley, a few acres not yet subdivided or cluttered with little stucco houses. The vacant lots stretched off to either side like drowned fields, brown and weedy and smelling the sour smell of earth too long wet.

"Come out," I said to the chauffeur.

"I — I don't understand."

"Come out. With your hands in front of you and empty."

He scrambled from under the wheel. "All right. I'm out. What now?"

"That," I said, and inclined my head toward what was sprawled inside the car's tonneau.

He turned and looked in. Under the soaked cling of his livery you could see his thin body going stiff with shock. He backed away from the limousine's open door and slowly faced me. His eyes were more protuberant than usual, and the muscles of his throat moved visibly.

"Holy Pete!" he said. "It's Gerald. Is — is he —"

"Dead, yes. Murdered."

"You — killed him? But why? Why?"

"Let's have none of that, Nixon. Accusing me isn't even clever. You can't get out of it that easily."

He breathed noisily. "What do you mean, I can't get out of it? Surely you don't think, you're not saying —"

"I'm saying you stabbed him."

"Oh, no! No!"

"You stabbed him before you went into the airport depot to get me."

"No," he repeated harshly. "No, you're wrong."

"The chances are he had recognized you. He knew you were the Edgar Nixon his uncle had helped send to prison. Maybe that was why he wanted me down here. He could have hired plenty of private detectives in Los Angeles, but they wouldn't do. He wanted me especially, because I could confirm your identification. I'd been the Cartwain Committee's special investigator in Washington and I was one man who would know you on sight."

He kept saying, "No, no," over and over, mechanically, like a phonograph record with a broken groove.

"You were afraid it was something like that, but you couldn't be sure. And so, to make sure, you murdered him before I could get together with him."

"No. No, you're wrong."

I put my face close to his. "You should have killed me, too," I said. "You might have got away with it, then. You overlooked a bet there. Or did you lose your nerve? Maybe one murder was all you could stomach. Is that how it was, Nixon?"

"No. He was alive when I left him in the car. He sent me into the station to get you. He gave me your name. He was alive, I tell you. How could he talk to me if he wasn't alive?"

"You're lying."

"No I'm not. If you didn't kill him, then it must have happened while you and I were talking in the airport waiting room. Look, Palmer, you've got to believe me —"

"But I don't," I said, and reached for the handcuffs I always carry in my back pocket. "Maybe you can convince the police, but I don't believe a word of it."

"You — you're going to turn me in?"

"Definitely."

His knees buckled under him and he went down, his back sliding along the side of the car. It was a smart trick. It threw me off guard. I thought he had fainted. Instead, he suddenly doubled forward and launched himself at me. He butted me in the stomach.

I didn't expect that and I wasn't prepared for it. Pain went through me like a sword and I dropped the handcuffs. I staggered and tried to keep from collapsing. My leg muscles cramped. Nixon came up and swung a punch at my chin. I couldn't parry it, couldn't get out of the way. His fist landed, hard and clean. . . .

Rain, beating against the nape of my neck, brought me back to consciousness. I was lying prone in the gutter behind the limousine, where Nixon had apparently dragged me after he had knocked me out. My stomach hurt like fury from being butted, and my jaw ached with a steady, constant throb like the pounding of drums. Feebly I pushed myself up on all fours, then sat for a moment on the low curb. It slowly dawned on me that I wasn't wearing my topcoat. It had been stripped off me.

My gun was gone, too. And so was Nixon.

Well, he would have needed the topcoat to cover his brown livery and make him less conspicuous for a getaway. As for the automatic, there was no telling what he might need that for. I could guess, though.

When I gathered enough strength I stood up. Swaying drunkenly, I moved to the car and peered inside. What I saw swept the last of the cobwebs out of my mind. Because what I saw was — nothing.

Gerald Cartwain's corpse had disappeared.

I pulled my pencil flashlight, sprayed its concentrated white glow all around me. Raindrops resembling falling gray bullets cut slantwise across the lightbeam, but there was no trace of the murdered man.

Swearing, I searched the weedy vacant lots beyond the sidewalk, trudged through soft spongy mud until I had covered the entire area.

I didn't find young Cartwain.

And I didn't find Edgar Nixon.

Back at the limousine, I discovered the ignition key still in the lock. I jammed myself under the wheel, pressed the starter. A smooth, surging flow of power answered my foot on the throttle paddle and I headed forward, making plans.

At a red and white Chevron station a mile farther on, I pulled in and took a quick look at the address on the cat's registration certificate. Then I asked the station attendant how to find that address. He got out a city map, put me straight.

Ten minutes later I gained my destination — a big neo-Colonial mansion perched on a knoll, surrounded by rolling lawn and reached by a graceful private driveway. I went up the driveway in second, my rear tires spitting gravel at the night.

Then I was vigorously thumbing the mansion's front doorbell.

My strap watch showed nine-thirty — not late enough for people to be in bed. But nobody answered my ring. Again I jabbed at the button and this time, after a long wait, the door opened.

"Yes, sir?" the girl who answered my ring asked.

SHE was a brunette in the black taffeta of a housemaid. Her skin was tawny, creamy; her face young but wise. The taffeta was tight over curves that were ample, though not lush. She looked at me with dark, impersonal eyes that gave you the impression of seeing more than they pretended to see.

"Is this Senator Cartwain's house?" I said.

"Yes, sir. Former Senator Cartwain," she added, as if to correct any mistaken notions I might have about his political status. "But he has retired for the night, sir."

"That's all right," I said, and pushed past her. "He'll be getting up again, soon enough. Right now, where's your phone?"

"Really, sir, I can't have this," the maid protested.

I had already noticed what I wanted, on the other side of the oak-paneled reception hall. I made for the telephone, picked it up, dialed 0 for operator and asked for Police Headquarters. Then I asked for Homicide, while the maid stared at me in growing bewilderment. "Homicide?" I said a moment later. "This is Don Palmer of the Schindemann Detective Agency, San Francisco. I'm calling from the residence of ex-Senator Cartwain near Van Nuys. That's right, Cartwain." I gave the address. "I want to report a murder. Cartwain's nephew and ward, Gerald. Stabbed. And his body stolen. I suggest you put out a radio reader for the Cartwain chauffeur — real name Edgar Nixon, but using an alias. About six-two, prominent eyes, thin build, wearing brown whipcord livery and a light tan topcoat which he took from me after knocking me unconscious. Yes, I'll be waiting here for your crew. Right."

I hung up.

Behind me there was a muffled thudding noise. I pivoted, saw that the taffeta-clad maid had crumpled to the floor. It was a genuine faint, I discovered when I loped over to her and stooped down. Her breathing was shallow and her dark eyes walled back so that only the whites showed.

There was a formal staircase to the left, and footfalls sounded on the upper steps. Then they reversed themselves swiftly and faded off. I kept trying to shake the maid awake, and the pattering click of high heels sounded again on the staircase. This time they came almost all the way down.

"Bring some water," I said, without glancing toward the stairs. "Or better still, brandy."

Then I looked up and saw a blonde girl standing on the fourth step from the bottom.

The long barreled .22 target automatic in her hands was pointed straight at my head.

CHAPTER III

A Muffled Scream

THE footfalls I had heard had been the blonde's, of course. They had started downstairs, had seen me leaning over the maid, had assumed I was a prowler and had gone back to get her gun.

"Whoever you are, put up your hands," she said now.

There was something vaguely familiar about her, some trick of expression or conformation of features I thought I ought to recognize, although I knew I had never seen her before. She wore a light blue negligee and matching satin mules, and her hair was the shining yellow of new gold, done in a braided cornet around her head.

She looked to be in her early twenties, or younger, and her mouth was compressed to a firm line — the only sign of emotion she allowed to show. Her eyes were bluer than the negligee, and as unwavering as the target pistol she aimed at me.

"Take it easy," I said. "This isn't what it seems to be."

"I told you to put your hands up. What have you done to Lora? If you've hurt her —"

Lora, then, was the maid's name. I lowered her, stepped back.

"Don't be ridiculous," I said. "I haven't done anything to her. She fainted when I phoned the police and accused your chauffeur of murder."

"Our chauffeur? You mean Judley?"

"If that's what he's been calling himself. He's really Edgar Nixon."

That didn't seem to mean anything. She frowned over it briefly and let it go.

"What's this you're saying about a murder?" she demanded.

"I think I'd sooner tell it to Senator Cartwain. Get him for me. Tell him Palmer wants to see him — Don Palmer of the Schindemann Detective Agency, San Francisco."

"He's asleep. Whatever you have to say, you can say it to me. I'm his niece."

I looked at her and suddenly knew why her face had seemed so puzzlingly familiar. It was a family resemblance.

"So you're Gerald Cartwain's sister."

"Yes. I'm Sylvia Cartwain."

"Put down that gun," I said gently as I could. "I've got bad news for you. Your brother is dead. He's the man your chauffeur murdered."

Her cheeks went pale and she leaned against the stair rail.

"You — you're joking."

"I wish I were."

She came down the last four steps, walked toward me.

"I don't believe you," she said tightly. "This is some monstrous lie." Then, when I shrugged, she said: "Where is his — where is the body?"

"I don't know."

"You don't know?"

I told her the whole story then, bluntly and quickly, and sparing her none of the details. I explained how Gerald had been knifed in the limousine, how Nixon had subsequently slugged me and escaped, somehow taking the corpse along with him.

"And now I'd better talk to your uncle," I finished.

Dully she indicated the staircase. "His room is the first one to the right on the second floor. I'll stay here and take care of Lora until the police come." She looked at the still unconscious maid. "Poor Lora. No wonder she fainted when she heard you accusing Judley."

"Nixon. Edgar Nixon. The Judley was an alias."

"It doesn't matter. Whoever he was, he and Lora were engaged to be married."

In itself, this was a piece of information that interested me, because it clashed with the pattern I had formed in my mind. It was a wrong note, jarring, having no place in the picture.

But beyond all that, I thought of Sylvia Cartwain herself as she told it to me. There was something fine and selfless about this blue-eyed girl, a quality of character as shining as her golden hair. Grief-stricken and stunned by the murder of her brother, she could find strength to subordinate that grief in her sympathy for a servant. In my work you don't often encounter people like that.

I suppressed an impulse to reach out, touch her hand. Instead I turned and went upstairs, found my way to the first door on the right in the upper hallway. I knocked, softly.

From the inside came what sounded like a low groan.

I rapped louder and the groan was repeated, distinctly. There was no question about it this time. I was hearing a man in trouble, in pain. I tried the knob, found the latch unfastened and gave the door a quick shove. The bedroom before me was dark, and once again came that deep-chested groan.

Fumbling at the wall just inside the door, I located a light switch. Flipping it gave me illumination from an overhead fixture. I stared toward a big four-poster bed across the room — and at the elderly man on it. A man bleeding from a stab wound.

He was former Senator Cartwain.

Shaggy and leonine in flannel pajamas, he lay massively on a crumpled pillow; a giant of a man with an unruly mop of cotton-white hair and a heavy-jarred face gone flabby in the jowls. Over his right eye socket there was a black patch. The left eye looked milky and rheumily opaque, leaving no doubt as to its blindness.

His pajama jacket was drawn up away from the shallow gash across his ribs, and the bed covers were stained bright crimson. He rolled and tried to sit up, turning his head and cocking his ear as I went toward him.

"You son of a witch," he said faintly. "So you've come back to finish me." He made a groping gesture. "Old and blind and weak as I am, if I could get my hands on you I'd —"

"Hold on a minute, Senator," I said, keeping out of his reach. "I'm not the one who stabbed you."

He strained his sightless face toward me. "I know that voice. You — you —"

"Don Palmer. I worked for your committee in the Senate. Investigator. Never mind that. Who knifed you?"

"Palmer," he said, ignoring my question. "Palmer. Yes. Yes, of course. Now I remember." His tone grew a little fuller, more resonant, with a hint of the oratorical quality he had put to such good use in his Washington days before his defeat for reelection. "Don Palmer. That profiteer case — and Nixon. Nixon, that sneaking, sniveling, cowardly —" The resonance faded, and Cartwain sagged against the pillow. "My side . . . ah-h-h —"

"Who did it?" I almost shouted at him. "Who stabbed you?"

"Bathroom," he mumbled, and flapped a hand in its direction. "Bandages — iodine. Do something — stop bleeding."

I raced from the room, raced back to the bed, and rolled the elderly man over on his side so I could get to the knife slash. One look told me it was painful but not serious. The blade had cut an ugly furrow but not a deep one.

I used a wet cloth to sponge away the blood, then poured iodine liberally. Cartwain winced, moaned. I slapped a pad of gauze against him, fastened it with strips of adhesive tape.

"Now will you tell me who knifed you?" I growled at him. "For heaven's sake, Senator, talk!"

"He came in — the window over there — must have climbed — up the portico."

"Who? Who was he?"

"I tried to — fight him off — but he cut me — and went back — out the window. Nixon — Edgar Nixon, lawyer — Washington trial. He called himself Judley, chauffeur, but I recognized him — when it was too late."

I sprang to the open window Cartwain kept mentioning. Rain was blowing over the sill in little gusts, and the carpet beneath was damp. Outside in the night there was a flat rectangle of roof with an ornamental balustrade around it. It was the roof of the portico below.

Nobody was on this roof, though, and if there had been footprints they had long since been washed off by the downpour.

It wouldn't be too difficult for a man to shinny up one of the portico's pillars, climb over the balustrade, come in the window and later get away by the same route; not too easy — but not too hard for a criminal with vengeance on his mind and murder in his heart.

"When was it?" I went back to the bed. "How long ago?"

"Five minutes — ten — I don't know. I tried to call out. I — wasn't able to make anybody hear." He broke in on himself, "What was that?"

I'd heard it, too — a muffled scream, then a thud.

It came from downstairs.

Then a door slammed.

I started out of the bedroom, fast.

"Stay where you are, Senator," I said over my shoulder, and I sped to the staircase, hurled myself downward three steps at a time.

A while ago, I had left the maid, Lora, unconscious on the floor of the reception hall with Sylvia Cartwain looking after her. Now the taffeta-clad brunette was gone and Sylvia lay sprawled in her place, an ugly bruise on her temple.

"Judley!" She managed to whisper as I ran to her. She still thought of the chauffeur by that name rather than Nixon. "He came in, took

Lora away. I tried to stop him — I tripped, fell."

Outside, a car motor roared alive and wheels spun on wet gravel, seeking traction.

Then the treads caught hold and the machine thundered off, gone before I could get to the front door.

I went sprinting out into the storm, trying to reconcile this new development with the things I had already learned. The driveway stretched in a graceful curving slant ahead of me from house down to street, but the limousine I had left parked there was no longer in view. I cursed myself for leaving the key in the ignition, then I realized that Nixon would probably have had a duplicate in any event.

A crazy urge took hold of me, an urge to dash in pursuit of the vanished car. In the grip of this blind, unreasoning impulse I lowered my head to the pelting rain and ran toward the rear of the grounds where there was a garage building with the servants' quarters above, like an old-fashioned plantation coach-house.

Surely, I reasoned, a family as well off as the Cartwains would own more than one automobile. After all, Marcus Cartwain was said to have retired from politics with a comfortable bank balance. Moreover, I recalled that young Gerald Cartwain and his sister had inherited a fair-sized fortune which was under their uncle's trusteeship, a fortune which likely would be entirely Sylvia's now that Gerald was dead.

I was right about the extra cars. I found two in the garage — a convertible and a station wagon, the latter spattered with rain-drops as if recently driven. Its instrument panel heat indicator needle, too, was up above the pin. But there was no key.

And none in the convertible, either.

By that time I had come to the realization that it didn't matter anyhow. Nixon had too big a start on me. There wasn't the remotest chance of overtaking him.

Dripping wet again, I went back into the mansion — and in a night full of surprises, I found still another surprise awaiting me there. A sort of combination den-library was located just off the reception hall on the left, and Sylvia Cartwain had recovered sufficient strength to totter in there, and to throw herself onto a leather upholstered davenport.

That wasn't what startled me, though. It was the sight of blind, hulking Marcus Cartwain bending over her, solicitously groping, trying awkwardly to comfort her.

CHAPTER IV

House of Menace

MARCUS Cartwain's vitality was enormous. He had put on a robe over his bloodstained flannel pajamas, and in spite of the weakening effects of I the stab wound in his side he had fumbled his way downstairs to be with his niece when she needed him most. His heavy face was gray, almost to the whiteness of his unruly hair, and he turned his head as I came into the room.

"Who's that?" he asked sharply.

"Don Palmer."

I went over to the davenport, looked down into the blonde girl's misty blue eyes.

"Are you all right, Sylvia?" I said. It didn't even occur to me that I should have called her Miss Cartwain.

"I — think so. I was j-just telling Uncle Marcus about — Gerald."

Cartwain's massive hands bailed into fists, impotently. "That swine Nixon!" Then, more calmly: "How did it happen?"

"Gerald came to meet me at the airport and sent Nixon in to get me. When he took me to the car, Gerald was already dead."

I repeated what I had previously explained to Sylvia — how the chauffeur had later knocked me senseless, and how he and his victim's body had been gone when I came to.

Cartwain's lips moved, almost soundlessly as they formed the question. "You've notified the police?"

"Yes."

"Then why aren't they here? Why don't they come?"

I glanced at my wrist-watch. "It was only ten or fifteen minutes ago that I phoned," I said. "They wouldn't despatch a radio car here. They probably short-waved every cruiser in the neighborhood to keep moving, keep on the lookout for Nixon. What they'll do is send us a squad from downtown Homicide, experts to ask questions, lift finger-prints, things like that."

"I don't like it," he said, peevishly querulous. "That Nixon must be a madman! First killing Gerald, then attacking me and coming down here, knocking Sylvia unconscious —"

She patted his arm. "I tripped, Uncle Marcus. He didn't knock me unconscious. He just grabbed Lora and said the police were after him, and they'd have to find a place to hide, start life all over again. I ran at him and stumbled. He never even touched me."

"He might have killed you. He must have planned to wipe out the whole family! And here we sit without police protection — me blind, not knowing when he may come sneaking in again to knife us in the back!"

"But Mr. Palmer is here, Uncle Marcus," Sylvia said. She smiled at me wanly.

I wondered if there might be a little irony in that. Thus far I had done little protecting of the Cartwains. I had arrived too late to save Gerald from death, the Senator from a wicked gash across the ribs, and Sylvia from a bump on the head. I seemed constantly to be one step behind these attacks, and I had a feeling that danger still hung over the big Colonial house, menacing, ominous and gathering force to strike again.

As long as this feeling persisted, I didn't intend to let the blonde girl out of my sight until her brother's murderer was under lock and key. Meanwhile, there was something I wanted to know.

"Senator Cartwain," I asked, "why did Gerald have my agency send me down here from San Francisco to see him? What was it he wanted me to investigate?"

His heavy face twisted bitterly. "It was something that I considered a lot of arrant nonsense. You see, I had received several threats —"

"Uncle Marcus!" Sylvia said. "You never told me!"

"No. Gerald didn't want to worry you, and as for me, I thought the whole thing was poppycock. A couple of anonymous phone calls, an unsigned letter — why, that sort of thing is commonplace to any man in public life. I've been threatened more times than I could count, and nothing ever came of them. How was I to know it was my own chauffeur getting ready for a spree of killing?"

"So Gerald wanted me to look into the threats, is that it?" I asked.

"Yes. And I suppose Nixon decided it was time to act, before you could trace the messages to him. So he stabbed Gerald, knifed me —"

"That's a lie!" a low, vibrant voice said from the doorway of the little den-library.

I whirled, stared. Then, slowly, I put my hands in the air.

WAS getting pretty tired of looking at guns being pointed at me by attractive young females, but I raised my hands anyhow. The girl in the doorway was Lora, and she had an expression in her unwavering dark eyes that warned me she would shoot if she was forced to.

On the davenport, Sylvia gasped and pressed against her uncle as if trying to shield him. I stood motionless, studying the brunette maid, and studying the stubby .32 automatic in her hand. It was my own Colt, the one Edgar Nixon had stolen from me when he had knocked me senseless on the way from the airport. Nixon must have given it to Lora.

But why was she back here in the house? What insane errand had brought her?

"You got away once," I said. "You should have stayed away."

Her body shivered under her rain-soaked, clinging black taffeta uniform.

"Stayed away on what? It takes money. I have some coming to me. I want it. I want my wages. They're past due."

"And Nixon's?"

"His, too."

"Was he afraid to come in himself?"

"You ought to know." She glared at me. "You're the one who accused him, framed him for something he didn't do. But don't think you'll make it stick. You won't even catch him. We ditched the limousine. And before I came back in here, we made sure the police hadn't arrived yet."

"They're here now," I said. "Right behind you."

Old as the trick was, she believed my lie and pivoted in panic. It was what I had hoped she would do.

The instant she moved, I launched myself at her. I didn't have to worry about the gun now. While it was pointed at me, I didn't stand a chance, but as soon as she started to turn it made the gamble worth trying. Springing, I got my hands on her shoulders. My weight bore her to the carpet, and I pinioned her there.

"Nice bait," I said.

She writhed, squirmed. "Let me g-go!" Then: "Bait?"

"I'm going to hold you," I said. "Maybe Nixon will get tired waiting. Maybe he'll start to worry. Maybe he'll come in to find out what happened to you. Then I'll have him."

Abruptly she stopped struggling. "No," she said in a curiously quiet voice. "Don't do that. You won't have to. He didn't kill Gerald."

"Didn't he?"

"No." She sighed wearily. "I did."

"Lora!" Sylvia Cartwain cried out sharply in a shocked voice.

Her uncle made a blind, groping gesture, his face registering disbelief; or perhaps it was disillusionment.

I had no illusions to lose. I got up, hauled the maid over to a chair, installed her and stood over her.

"So you murdered Gerald. Why? What was your motive?"

"He promised to marry me. He reneged."

"Wait," I said. "You and Nixon were engaged."

"Nixon can worry," she said cynically. Too cynically. "It was Gerald I wanted. It was Gerald I thought I had. At least he had me. The heel. He could twist a woman around his finger. He made me believe he loved me. Me, a servant, a maid. And him rich, high society, a Senator's nephew. Or anyhow a former Senator's. I guess it flattered me. Anyhow I fell for his line."

"And Nixon?"

"I was just stringing him along for kicks." She was hard about it. She overdid the hardness.

"So when it came time for wedding bells, Gerald backed out," I said. "Is that the way of it?"

"That was how it was. And when he went to the airport tonight to meet you, I followed him: I waited until he was alone, sitting so high and mighty in the limousine. I killed him."

"You say you followed him. How?"

"I drove."

"In one of the other family cars?"

"Yes. You think I've got a car of my own on my wages? Wages two months overdue?"

"Which car did you drive?" I said.

"The —" She hesitated. "The convertible."

I picked up my gun from the floor where she had dropped it. I beckoned Sylvia Cartwain, and when the blonde got up from the couch I handed her the weapon.

"I'm going to phone the police and see what's delaying them. Keep Lora covered with this."

"You don't have to keen me covered," Lora said. "I'll take my medicine, just so you keep Nixon out of it. He's innocent."

AS IT developed, I didn't have to phone Headquarters, either. Just as I went toward the reception hall phone, the doorbell rang. I answered it and admitted three plainclothes detectives out of Homicide. They had a fourth man with them, a thin man in a wet, badly fitting topcoat — my topcoat, covering a brown, soggy whipcord livery.

The law had caught up with Edgar Nixon.

One of the detectives was a man I had known in my earlier days on the Coast, before the war — a sinewy little lieutenant named Otto Kleinstadt. He had a face as narrow and sharp as an ax, eyes like gimlets.

"Hello, Palmer," he said. Then he indicated his prisoner. "Know him?"

"Yes. Nixon."

"Thought so. We caught him sulking around the grounds and he matched the description you phoned in. Looks like a nice quick clean-up, eh? No chase, no trouble at all. Funny, nabbing him here at the house. From what you told us, I figured he'd be long gone and far away."

Nixon's shoulder twitched with nervous tic he had. "Now listen," he said. "I was railroaded once. It's not going to happen again."

"So you were railroaded," I said. "By the Cartwain Committee. Actually by Marcus Cartwain. That's why you hated him, hated his whole family. You got this job as his chauffeur for one reason only — revenge. A chance to get even. You knew he wouldn't recognize you because he was blind. You were waiting for an opportunity to start a family massacre."

"It's a lie. I told you I'd put all that out of my mind. When I met Lora I changed. All I wanted was to marry, settle down, forget the past."

"Lora?" Otto Kleinstadt said. "Who's Lora?"

"The maid here," I told him.

"I'm no killer," Nixon said. "I didn't murder Gerald Cartwain. I didn't do it."

"But you knocked me unconscious," I said.

"I admit that."

"And stole my coat and my gun."

"You think I wanted to stick around while you framed me?"

"And you disposed of Gerald's body somehow," I said.

"Down a storm drain. It will turn up at the outfall, or Ballona Creek. I was a little bit crazy to do that, I guess. But I wasn't thinking straight. I was cornered. Anyhow I know I didn't murder him."

"I believe you," I said.

With that, he blinked at me as if doubting his ears. Lieutenant Kleinstadt blinked, too.

"What the devil, Palmer!" he exploded. "You said he was guilty!"

"That was before Lora confessed."

Nixon stiffened. "What?"

"You made a mistake letting her back here for her wages." I smiled him. "She walked into trouble she couldn't cope with."

Then I took him into the den-library with Kleinstadt and the other two headquarters men trooping along behind.

CHAPTER V

A Good Trick — That Didn't Work

FORMER Senator Cartwain was sitting on the davenport with his head to one side the way a blind man always does, using his ears for eyes. Sylvia stood against a wall, leaning tiredly, but keeping my little automatic trained on the maid who was still in the chair where I had left her.

Nixon took in the scene.

"Lora," he said harshly, "Palmer says you confessed you killed Gerald."

"Yes." She was calm. "Yes, I confessed."

"But why — why do a thing like that!"

"To save you from the lethal chamber, of course," I said. "What other reason would she have for lying like that? She loves you. A woman will make any sacrifice for a man she loves."

Lora's dark eyes met mine reluctantly. "I didn't lie. I murdered Gerald Cartwain."

"Stop being noble," I told her. "Your story was full of holes. You overacted it. The main discrepancy was, you said you followed the limousine to the airport by driving in the Cartwain convertible. I happen to know the convertible is as dry as a bone. It hasn't been out in the rain at all. You should have said the station wagon. I might have believed you then, because it's wet and its motor is still warm. You guessed the wrong car."

Nixon went toward her. "Lora! You mean you were actually willing to let them convict you of murder — for me?"

"I wouldn't have gone all the way through with it," she answered him moodily. "I just wanted to give you a chance to get away." Her lower lip trembled. "I was playing for time. I couldn't stand the thought of them strapping you in a chair and — and starting the gas."

Suddenly her reserve broke. She wept, quietly and with big racking sobs. He touched her shoulder.

"You thought they'd convict me, Lora? Because I wanted to run away, you thought I was guilty?"

"Yes."

"I'm innocent, Lora. I didn't kill Gerald."

I took my gun out of Sylvia's hand and backed toward the doorway.

"He's telling the truth, Lora," I said. "He did a lot of foolish things, such as hitting me, getting rid of the corpse, coming here and taking you away, then letting you come back for your wages. He doesn't stack high for brains, but he didn't kill Gerald."

Everybody was staring at me except Marcus Cartwain, who couldn't see.

"Somebody else followed Gerald and Nixon in the limousine," I said. "Somebody who used the station wagon and waited until Nixon left Gerald alone and then knifed him. I'm aiming at the killer," I added, and pointed my .32 at blonde Sylvia Cartwain.

I had all the puzzle's pieces neatly put together, in my mind at least, so that the pattern was clear and plain. But much of it still needed proving, which wouldn't be easy.

Sylvia stood speechless as my gun menaced her. Nixon and Lora breathed audible gasps. Otto Kleinstadt, flanked by his two plainclothes colleagues, started moving toward the golden-haired girl, and over on the davenport her uncle dabbed at his milkily opaque left eye with a mussed linen handkerchief while adjusting and tugging at the black patch over the right one. He dislodged the patch briefly, snapped it hastily back in place.

"Much obliged, Senator," I said. "Eh? What? What?"

I shifted my automatic to cover him. "Thanks for the confession. Thanks for helping me prove you murdered your nephew."

"I murdered my nephew? Are you insane? How could I have killed him? I'm blind."

"Blind only in the left eye," I said. "Your right eye has perfect vision, barring that patch you wear over it. That's why I used a little trick just now, to make you give yourself away. I announced that I was aiming at the killer, but I mentioned no names. It caught you off guard. In your own conscience, you knew you were guilty. You wondered if you were the one I was accusing.

"With the patch on your good eye, you couldn't see where I was pointing my automatic. Maybe at you, maybe at someone else in the room. You had to know, you had to find out. So you dabbed at your blind eye with a handkerchief and managed to move the patch from the other one, just for an instant. Just long enough to see that Sylvia was the person under my gun.

"Then you let the patch drop back into position. I was watching you, waiting for you to make that move. I expected you to. And you did."

"You're out of your head!"

I stepped close to him. "Am I?" Then I yanked away the patch, and his perfectly sound right eye glared at me maniacally. "Look at me, Senator," I said. "Take a good look and tell me now if I'm crazy."

"Curse you — curse you!"

"Uncle Marcus!" Sylvia wailed, and the others in the room involuntarily stirred and muttered like a shocked audience at some corrupt melodrama. Cartwain cursed me again, thickly.

"I think it must have been a long-range plan," I said to him. "Something you plotted months ago, when your left eye went blind. With a patch on the right eye you could pretend complete blindness. That was the start of your murder plan."

"Curse you, curse you, curse you!" he repeated.

"Next came Edgar Nixon," I said. "Either accidentally or by design, you'd learned he was out of prison and in Los Angeles, jobless. You got rid of your former chauffeur, then, and somehow managed to get the news to Nixon that the position was open. You also made sure he heard that you were blind, so that he'd feel safe from recognition if he applied for the job. Clever psychology, Senator. You counted on him applying. As a political expedient you'd ruined him in Washington and he had good cause to hate you, to be vengeful. That's why you wanted him in your household. It made him a logical fall guy for the murder you were planning."

He swore at me again, over and over.

"I first suspected you when I found you stabbed in your bed," I told him. "You accused Nixon, said you had recognized him. How could a blind man recognize anybody? That was a minor slip of the tongue, a lie told blunderingly, a false note that started me thinking. And your wound was shallow, as it might be if self-inflicted, whereas Gerald had been stabbed once and deeply enough to cause death. If the murderer could kill Gerald with one stroke of knife, how could he possibly do such an incomplete job on you, a helpless blind man? It wasn't in character for a killer, but it was characteristic of stage-dressing. Of fakery."

He seemed to shrink against the davenport's leather upholstery. He looked a thousand years old.

"And if you'd been really blind," said, "how could you know a man came in your window? How could you tell? There was something else, too. You claimed you had been attacked five or ten minutes before. But the carpet under the window was barely damp. The way the rain was coming in, the carpet would have been soaking wet in five or ten minutes. That meant you had opened the window a mere moment before I knocked on your door. You lied. Everything you'd told me was a lie, including that wild yarn about receiving anonymous threats. I don't believe there ever were any threats. That was a story you cooked up to keep me from guessing Gerald's real reason for asking my agency to send me down here."

"His real reason?"

I nodded. "I'm theorizing now. Something Lora said tipped me to it. You were supposed to be well-fixed if not wealthy. Gerald and Sylvia had a fair-sized fortune, and you were trustee of their estate. But the maid's wages were past due. So were Nixon's. Where was all the money you were supposed to have? What had happened to Gerald's and Sylvia's inheritance? Maybe you had been embezzling, gambling, dissipating everything. Maybe Gerald's suspicions were aroused. Maybe he demanded an accounting that you didn't dare give him. Maybe that was why you planned to kill him. He was on to you."

"Curse you," Cartwain said monstrously. "Curse you to perdition."

"So finally he decided to send for me, hire me to investigate your finances. That brought it to a head. You're the one who drove the station wagon tonight, followed the limousine, waited until your nephew was alone and then stabbed him. Perhaps you intended to kill Sylvia, too. I caught you groping over her, pretending to comfort her. Were you going to break her neck and pin that on Nixon, too? Then you wouldn't have had to give an estate accounting to anybody."

Cartwain put a hand down between two of the leather cushions.

"Come with me to Hades, Palmer," he said, and brought up the long-barreled .22 target gun that I had last seen in Sylvia's hand.

She must have left it on the davenport when she rested there, earlier. And Cartwain had it now. He snapped a shot at me.

He got me in the right arm. Then, behind me, Otto Kleinstadt fired his service .38 and destroyed the only good eye Marcus Cartwain had.

Where the eye had been, there was now a bright red hole.

"Save the State the cost of a trial," Kleinstadt said, almost apologetically. Then, to Sylvia, "Sorry, Miss Cartwain. I guess I didn't realize I was such a good marksman. But you'd have been out an uncle in the long run, anyhow."

She didn't seem to hear him, didn't even look at the former Senator's corpse. She came running to me.

"Mr. Palmer, your arm — your poor arm! It's bleeding!"

It was nice to know she cared. It was an incongruous time for such notions, but I kept thinking she was probably poor, now. Her estate had been squandered if my theories were correct. And then I thought that a private detective makes pretty fair money. Maybe I would never afford a chauffeur and maid like Nixon and Lora, but I could take care of a wife. I could take very good care of a wife with hair the color of new gold.

I stopped daydreaming. That was looking too far into the future.

"It's all right, Sylvia," I said. "Don't worry about my arm. One of these days I'll get in touch with you. I'll be as good as new."

KILL THAT HEADLINE

DEFTLY-APPLIED rouge couldn't mask the chalky pallor of her cheeks. Her mouth was a tremulous crimson blossom against deathly whiteness. She walked into the *Morning Planet* city-room unsteadily, like a person drunk — or drugged.

Ken Fitch, city editor on the night side, happened to glance up from the headline he was readying — a headline that would split the town wide open. Less than two hours ago he'd had a visit from Cokey Joe Breen, who had spilled the facts behind that headline — for a cash consideration. And now, seeing the blond girl approaching, Ken Fitch stiffened with surprise.

"Letha Starke!" he muttered.

She came falteringly toward the raised platform where his desk was situated — the dais from which he could keep a watchful eye on reporters, rewrite men, and copy-desk slaves under his charge. Pendant green-shaded incandescents sent reflected glints of light shining against the oncoming girl's metallic yellow hair, revealing every perfectly-spaced wave of her artistic coiffure. Her lush curves were stressed by an expensive mink coat drawn tightly about her, so that each step she took revealed the bold, arrogant lines of her slinky figure.

"Ken — !" she whispered as she gained the platform.

He frowned. He didn't get up from his chair. A swift, roving glance informed him that every masculine eye in the room was appraisingly fastened on his visitor. Her blatant beauty always did that to the men she encountered. Typewriters had ceased clattering; there was only the steady, spaced click of teletype printers to mar the admiring hush that had fallen over the night crew.

Confronting Ken Fitch, the girl's back was turned to the others. Her pale blue eyes wavered to meet his gaze. "Ken — !" she whispered again, pleadingly.

He flushed, conscious of the knowing grins on the faces of his subordinates. "Well, Letha, what's on your mind?" His tone pointedly lacked cordiality. He cast a look toward a desk at the far end of the room — Molly Kildare's desk.

Molly Kildare was petite, red-haired, wholesomely feminine and a crack reporter. Also, she was Ken Fitch's fiancée; they were to be married next month. He didn't like the idea of Molly seeing him talking to Letha Starke. Molly knew of his infatuation for Letha five years ago — an infatuation he had long since outgrown. Would Molly misunderstand this present meeting?

But she wasn't paying any attention. She was pawing through a desk-drawer as if searching for mislaid notes. Apparently she hadn't even noticed Letha Starke's entrance into the city room. Ken was relieved.

Again he stared up into the blue eyes of the blonde girl. Irritated, he repeated: "What's on your mind, Letha?"

"I'm in trouble, Ken. Ghastly trouble. I need you — desperately."

His lips took on a wry twist. "So you've come back to me after five years. After giving me the frigid air. After taking me for my bankroll and then handing me the gate. Now you say you need me. Rather ironic, don't you think?"

"You don't understand, Ken. This is different. I'm not asking you to forgive me for what I did to you. That's buried. I was a fool — and I learned my lesson. Too late. But now I've got nobody else to turn to. If you don't help me, they'll s-send me to the electric chair!"

He was startled. He crushed out his cigarette. "What do you mean by that?"

"Ken — I just killed a man." She unfastened the fur coat and permitted it to fall open.

He choked back his sharp exclamation of surprise. She was wearing an evening gown of white satin that adhered like a caress to her lovely body. She was magnificently contoured. Her hips swelled lyrically against the clinging silk, and her snowy bosom was daringly revealed by deep-slashed décolletage. One shoulder-strap dangled, torn as if in some struggle. The front of the gown was splotched and spattered with reddish brown stains. He guessed their meaning before she spoke.

"Blood, Ken," the yellow-haired girl whispered as she closed the coat about her.

He regained composure. "So you killed a man."

"Yes. In my apartment. An hour ago."

"Who was he?"

"I — I don't know, Ken."

"You don't know? Then what the devil was he doing in your apartment?"

She reddened painfully. "I met him on a wild party this evening. He insisted on taking me home. I didn't think he'd —"

"Wait a minute, Letha. You're lying. I don't believe you."

"Oh, I know." Her smile was rueful and forced, without mirth. "You don't believe I'd ever sink low enough to invite a total stranger to my apartment. Well, Ken, you're quite wrong. I was drunk. And I thought I didn't care. The steps always lead downward — eventually. To the gutter."

He scowled thoughtfully. "What about your pal DeWitt Ragan? I thought he was footing your bills?" Asking that, Ken casually covered the headline and the typewritten sheets on his desk — the story he'd been writing when Letha appeared. The story given to him by Cokey Joe Breen.

He didn't want Letha to see that headline — because, oddly enough, it dealt with this very DeWitt Ragan now under discussion.

The blond girl said: "Ragan? He ditched me more than a month ago — the rat."

That struck Ken as sardonically amusing. It was funny to hear her call anybody a rat for ditching her — considering how she herself had ditched Ken, more years ago than he cared to remember. He said: "So Ragan gave you the bum's rush. And since then you've been entertaining strangers. And tonight you croaked one. Why?"

"He was a b-beast. I discovered I couldn't bring myself to . . . let him maul me."

"Hm-m-m. So what happened?"

"I tried to get him to leave quietly. But he got nasty. There was a struggle. I p-picked up a brass candlestick and hit him over the head. . . ." Her knees seemed to grow wabbly under her. "Ken — Ken — you've got to help me get rid of that corpse; I d-don't want to go to the chair!"

He came to a sudden decision. "Okay. I'll see what can be done." He scribbled some instructions to Biff McQuaide, his assistant; called McQuaide to the desk and left him in charge. Ken and the blonde girl walked toward the exit.

They had to pass Molly Kildare's desk. Ken stopped for a moment while Letha swept onward. He leaned down over the petite red-haired girl. "Be back in a little while, honeysweet. Wait for me."

Molly's eyes were deep violet pools of worry. "You're going out with that Starke woman?"

He grinned and nodded. "Not jealous, are you?"

"N-no . . ." Molly's adorably piquant face wore a troubled expression; her firm little bosom rose and fell swiftly, as if with inner tumult. She laid a hand gently on Ken's arm. "No. I'm not jealous. But something tells me you're walking into danger, Ken. Intuition —"

He brushed her lips tenderly with his mouth. "Don't be foolish, sweetheart. I'll be okay." He went out.

Downstairs, Letha Starke had a taxi waiting. In the tonneau's darkness she sat close to him, so that he could feel the warm, insinuating softness of her, impinging on his own muscular solidarity. There'd been a time, long ago, when his blood would have run faster at her nearness. His arm would have stolen around her waist in a crushing embrace; he would have buried his face in the perfectly-coifed masses of her yellow hair and then searched demandingly with his lips for her waiting, sensuous mouth. . . .

But not now. That was irrevocably ended. He sat quietly, almost serenely. He paid no attention to her coquettish challenge.

She seemed to sense his indifference. "You hate me, don't you, Ken?"

"No. I passed that stage, years ago."

"Then why are you so cold to me?"

"Listen, Letha. I happen to be in love with someone else. The real thing this time. A girl named Molly Kildare. I'm going to marry her next month."

"She's the one you kissed, back in the office? The red-haired one?"

He smiled. "Yes. So you were watching?"

"I was. I couldn't h-help it. She's sweet, lovely. Oh, Ken — if only things had been different! If I hadn't been such a silly, stupid fool, five years ago . . . !"

"Forget it," he told her.

"Ken — why are you so willing to help me now, if you don't care anything about me?"

He shrugged. "Maybe because I'm a sentimentalist. Here we are at your place." He helped her from the cab and paid the tariff.

They went upstairs to the second floor of the building. She unlocked her door and switched on the living-room's lights.

"The c-corpse is in here. . . ." she whispered. She took his arm and led him into her boudoir, clinging closely to him as they stepped over the threshold. She pointed to her mussed bed.

A man lay there, face upward; his glazed eyes staring blindly at the ceiling. His skull was crushed in. Blood and smeared brains stained the pillows.

Ken Fitch drew a sharp breath. "Good God — !" he rasped. "Cokey Joe Breen!"

And then something smashed down on his head, from behind. Something that thudded viciously against his temple as he wheeled around. Something that sent blasting fires of agony searing into his brain.

He pitched forward. The floor seemed to come up and strike him on the face.

Over the roaring in his ears he heard a man's voice snarling: "Got the lousy snoop!" Then came Letha Starke's callous, amused tinkle of laughter.

Ken struggled drunkenly to his knees, felt blood running down his cheek from the cut in his scalp where the blackjack had laid the flesh open. He blinked back his daze as he stared up into a man's leering features.

"DeWitt Ragan . . . !" he mumbled thickly.

His tuxedoed attacker, president of the Ragan Construction Company, snarled: "Right. And if you start anything, I'll feed you another dose of the same."

A surging seethe of fury entered Ken's soul. He bounced to his feet as anger gave him new strength. He lunged at Ragan; bashed a knotted fist at the contractor's snarling mouth. The blow connected solidly. Ragan's gums spouted blood like squeezed sponges, and he spat out broken shards of teeth as he staggered back. Fitch followed him, battered at him —

Blam!

Another man had leaped into the room. He had a reversed automatic in his hand. He thudded it against Ken's head savagely. And this time the lights went completely out for the newspaperman.

WHEN he opened his eyes, he was trussed to a chair in the living-room. DeWitt Ragan was bloodily grinning at him, his arm encircling Letha Starke's supple waist. Over on the divan sat the man whose blow had stretched Ken Fitch unconscious. Ken recognized the fellow as Ragan's chauffeur.

Ragan said: "You lousy sap! So you wanted to help Letha, eh? Too bad, sucker. Because I'm dealing the cards my way from now on."

"Meaning —?"

"You know damned well what I mean. Cokey Joe Breen spilled his guts to you tonight about my city hall contract for the new bridge across East Bay. You figured to pin back my ears by running a scoop on the graft I'm getting."

Ken blinked. "So you caught Breen and made him squeal."

"He squealed, all right. And now he's dead. Which is what you'll be — unless you kill that story about me."

Squirming against his fetters, Ken rasped: "Have another guess, Ragan. That story runs in tomorrow morning's edition. You can't stop it."

"No. But you can. And you will."

The newspaperman laughed shortly. "Go ahead and do your damnedest, you filthy crook. The minute you turn me loose and send he back to the *Planet* office, I'll blast hell out of you. Not only for graft — but for murder." He glanced significantly toward the boudoir, where Cokey Joe Breen's body lay.

Ragan approached the chair. He raised his fist, smashed it to Ken's jaw. He snarled: "Shut up!"

Ken shook his head jerkily to clear away the blur. Then he grinned again, "You think you can scare me by beating me up? Nuts, Ragan! You're a bigger fool than I thought you were."

The contractor's scowl was savage with wrath. "Hero stuff. Maybe you won't feel so brave when your red-haired girl friend ankles in here."

Ken stiffened. A sudden icy shock trickled down his spine. "What — !"

"Yeah." Ragan laughed triumphantly. "I phoned the *Planet* while you were knocked out. I imitated your voice. I talked to your sweetie. I asked her to come up here right away. She's on her way now."

Flooding, impotent rage churned in Ken Fitch's heart. Molly Kildare — walking straight into a trap! Sweet, unsuspecting Molly — heading innocently into murderous danger! "You wouldn't dare — !" he shouted.

Ragan's lips peeled back from his broken teeth. "No? Guess again. I'll bet that's her now!" he added as a knock sounded on the door.

Ken twisted ineffectually against the ropes that held him. He raised his voice. "Molly — for God's sake — run!" he shouted hoarsely.

But Ragan's ape-like chauffeur had already launched himself at the door, jerked it open. He reached out, made a grab — and dragged Molly into the room.

The red-haired girl went white as she clawed at her captor. She saw Ken Fitch tied to the chair, and her violet eyes widened in terror. "Ken — !"

The chauffeur slapped her viciously across the mouth, his hard palm splatting like the report of a gun. "Button your kisser, babe!" he growled.

She staggered; then she renewed her struggles. She kicked at the thug; tried to pound his face with her tiny fists. He twined his fingers in her auburn hair; jerked her head far back. He struck her again; tried to carry her across the room.

She fought him like a tigress. His hand caught in the neck of her frock, ripping it from one shoulder. She wailed and tried to cover the flesh exposed under the torn material. Her attacker forced her to the divan and bounced her against the cushions. The hem of her skirt flew up past her stocking-tops. There was a flash of smooth, ivory skin.

Beaten, cowed, she crouched shivering on the sofa as the chauffeur pinned her wrists. He grunted: "Be good or I'll sock you again, sister."

Letha Starke interrupted. "No, you needn't bother. I want that pleasure for myself. String her up to the chandelier."

Ken Fitch's throat went dry. "You damned fiends — you can't get away with this!"

Ragan snarled: "Shut up, snoop. Don't make me slug you unconscious. I want you to be awake — so you can see what's happening." He helped his chauffeur bind Molly's wrists with a length of clothesline. Then they lifted her to the center of the room; fastened the rope to the overhead lighting-fixture.

The red-haired girl dangled there, moaning; her little feet barely touching the floor. Ragan took off his leather belt and handed it to Letha Starke. "Okay, kiddo. Have your fun."

Letha stepped forward, prepared to lash Molly with the strap.

Ken Fitch shouted again. "No — for God's sake — !"

The yellow-haired woman laughed; brought the leather belt swishing venomously in a circling arc. Splat! The belt stung into Molly's smooth flesh, left a red weal on white, where its end touched her bare shoulder. Splat! Again the improvised whip licked out. Molly whimpered —

Ken roared: "Quit! Stop it! I'll kill that damned story! I promise!"

But Molly Kildare's voice halted his outcries. "No, Ken. Let them go ahead and whip me. If it's something that should be printed — print it!" Her proud eyes swept the room. She faced Letha Starke. "Go ahead. Help yourself."

Letha started to strike once more. But Ragan grabbed the strap. "Nix, kiddo. I've got a better scheme."

"What do you mean?"

He untied the red-haired girl; carried her to the divan. Then he winked at his chauffeur. "All right, guy. I've been watching you. You've had your eye on this dish ever since she ankled in. Well — she's yours!"

Helpless fury scalded Ken Fitch's soul. "You rats — you lousy, stinking swine'! You can't — you wouldn't —"

Ragan slugged him in the mouth, silenced him. He tasted the salt tang of his own blood from split lips. Raging, struggling vainly against the cords that held him to the heavy chair, he saw the chauffeur go to the divan and lean over Molly's cringing form. . . .

She whimpered — once. Then the thug had her in his arms; glued his thick lips to her averted mouth.

Wildly Ken shouted: "Stop! I give in! I swear it! I'll kill the story — I'll do anything you say!" And this time Molly gave him no contradiction. . . .

Ragan grunted: "Okay. Let up, Terry."

The chauffeur released Molly; growled sullen reluctance as he swung around.

Ragan was at work on Ken's bonds. He snarled: "Listen, Mister. I'm giving you this one chance. You're going back to the *Planet* office. You're going to destroy every bit of the stuff Cokey Joe Breen gave you. I'm sending Terry with you — in case you try any funny stuff. He'll have a roscoe, and he hasn't got any scruples about using it."

Ken Fitch was desperately sparring for precious minutes. "Your gorilla won't have to shoot me, Ragan. I give you my word I'll destroy that story. Nobody knows about it except me. All I ask is that you let Molly go —"

The contractor said: "Nuts, boyfriend. The jane stays right here — until you come back with proof that you killed that headline. I'm giving you thirty minutes to get the job done. If you aren't back here by then — well, something damned unpleasant will happen to your girl friend. Gargle that one."

Ken stole a glance at Ragan's wrist-watch; saw that he'd been away from his city-desk five minutes less than a full hour. His heart began to hammer against his chest. Five minutes to go. . . . It seemed like a bleak eternity stretching out before him. He knew that he didn't dare leave this apartment until that five minutes had snailed by. . . .

Time! He had to gain it somehow. Ragan had already untied the ropes at his ankles; was now at work on his wrist-bonds. The contractor was working swiftly. Too swiftly.

And then Ken was free. He swayed to his feet. Ragan stood before him. Over by the door was Terry, the chauffeur — with his fist in his coat pocket and an ominous bulge that told of an automatic's muzzle poking the cloth. Letha Starke hovered near the davenport, keeping guard over Molly. . . .

"Get Going!" Ragan rasped.

Ken Fitch Took a wild, desperate chance. He tensed his sinews — and went smashing at the contractor like a stone from a catapult.

The move took Ragan by surprise; bowled him backward. Ken's fist lashed out like pistons; impacted against his enemy's jaw. He felt the jarring thud all the way to his own shoulders.

Ragan's head snapped back as if hinged. He went down.

Letha Starke screamed a gutter oath. The chauffeur came slamming across the room, his gun drawn. He yelled: "Stand back, Miss Starke — I'll plug him!"

Ken dived for the floor. He hit the carpet just beyond where Ragan had fallen. He grabbed for the unconscious contractor; used the man's limp form for a shield. "Go ahead and shoot!" he panted. "You'll kill your boss if you do!"

The thug's finger relaxed its pressure on the trigger of the automatic. He darted sidewise, seeking a clear aim at the newspaperman. Ken rolled, keeping Ragan in front of him —

But he forgot Letha Starke. She darted in, flung herself on Ragan, dragged him aside. Ken was wholly exposed to the chauffeur's weapon, now. He scrambled to his feet, zigzagging. With a blow of his fist he sent the blond woman sprawling. She went down in a flurry of white satin skirt; her chiffon legs kicked and thrashed as she landed.

The chauffeur jumped as Letha landed at his feet. He swerved around her. That was Ken's chance. He sailed full at his antagonist before the man could again raise his gun to firing position.

They met with a thumping crash of flesh against flesh, brawn against brawn.

From the divan, Molly Kildare screamed: "Ken — look out! Ragan's getting up!"

And then Fitch smashed his right fist square into the chauffeur's mouth. The fellow sagged; went to his knees. The automatic dropped from his hand. Ken lashed out with his foot; kicked the thug brutally. The chauffeur doubled over, retching and holding his middle.

Whirling, Ken saw Ragan coming at him — with a gun.

It was too late to scoop up the chauffeur's weapon. Too late to do anything — except brace himself for Ragan's bullet. The contractor's narrow eyes gleamed with murderous malice. He grated: "You asked for it—now take it!" He squeezed his trigger.

But even as his gun vomited flame, the apartment's door crashed inward. A knot of uniformed men came thundering into the room. Ragan's shot went wild; a slug screamed past Ken Fitch's ear. And then the police were grappling with DeWitt Ragan, disarming him, handcuffing him. They jerked the fallen chauffeur to his feet,manacled him to his employer. And they lifted Letha Starke; pinioned her.

Ken Fitch saw his *Planet* assistant, Biff McQuaide, in the thick of things. He yelled: "Biff — thank God you got here before it was too late!"

McQuaide grinned. "You should have made it thirty minutes instead of an hour, from the looks of things."

DeWitt Ragan was snarling, fighting his handcuffs. "What the hell — who — how —"

Ken's eyes gleamed bale fully. "You aren't quite smart enough, Ragan. In the first place, I knew Letha's story was a lie. I knew it the minute she walked into the *Planet* city-room. I realized she was trying to trick me, trap me. That was obvious enough."

The contractor stared. "You — you knew?"

"Yes. Letha said she'd killed a man, in a struggle. She showed me bloodstains on her dress. Okay. The blood was genuine. But there hadn't been any struggle. Because her hair wasn't mussed!"

Ragan stiffened.

Ken went on. "You heard me. Her coiffure was a work of art. Not a single wave was out of place. So I knew her yarn about a struggle was all phony. So was her torn dress. So was everything else she told me.

"I figured she was lying when she claimed you'd thrown her over. If she was so damned hard up that she had to entertain strangers, what was she doing with that expensive mink coat? Nothing added up right. So I guessed that she was trying to lure me into a trap.

"Who'd want to trap me? Nobody but you — on account of the story

I was going to run about you. Well, I deliberately walked into your scheme, Ragan. Because I wanted to find out the truth about you. I wanted to make sure Cokey Joe Breen had handed me a right steer when he gave me that information about your grafting.

"I went haywire in just one detail. I didn't expect you to conk me and lure Molly Kildare up here. You almost won out by doing that. Almost — but not quite. Because when I left the *Planet* office I scribbled a note for McQuaide, my assistant. I instructed him to wait an hour — and then, if I hadn't returned, he was to come to this apartment with a squad of cops."

Ragan wilted. "I'll take a plea. They won't fry me . . ." he drooled. "I've got influence. . . ."

An officer jerked him toward the door. "Nuts, buddy. Get goin'."

Slowly the room cleared. One bluecoat was left to stand guard over Cokey Joe Breen's corpse in the adjoining boudoir. Ken Fitch slipped over to the divan; lifted Molly Kildare in his arms.

She clung to him fiercely. "Oh, Ken. . . ." she whispered.

He kissed her. He said: "Let's not wait until next month, honey-sweet. What do you say?"

She wrapped her soft arms around his neck and held up her mouth for another kiss. It was all the answer he needed.

WAR PLANS DIVIDED

THE muffled voice said: "We've got your wife, Paxton. And if you don't believe that, listen." Then, after a pause, Barbara was on the line.

"Nick, darling, they k-kidnaped me as I was coming out of the movie theater —" She stopped talking, as if a hand had been clapped over her mouth.

I jammed the receiver against my ear until the hard rubber circle was a grinding pain there. But I kept my tone steady. I mustn't go hysterical, I told myself. Melodramatics wouldn't help.

"Okay." I said. "You've got my wife. Who are you and what's the payoff?"

"Never mind who we are," the muffled voice told me. "The payoff will be the plans of your new Paxton-Leland radio remote-control for bombing planes. We know they're ready for Washington, and we want them. By midnight."

"Otherwise?" I asked quietly.

"You guess," the voice said. Then I heard Barbara again:

"They say they'll k-kill me, Nick!"

And the man's voice came back to add: "We mean it, Paxton. Think it over."

I didn't have to think it over. I already knew what my answer must inevitably be. Barbara came first, because I loved her. Barbara's safety came ahead of my friendship for Todd Leland, my partner; ahead of my loyalty to my country. I said:

"You win, whoever you are. Tell me what I'm to do."

The voice seemed pleased. "For one thing, you're not to contact the police. You understand that?"

"I understand that."

The voice said: "You are to bring the plans — both sets of them — to room 210, the Norcross Hotel, Burbank. That is all."

"By midnight?"

"Not one minute later. Unless you want to be a widower."

I looked desperately at my wrist-watch. "But it's eleven o'clock now," I argued swiftly. "An hour isn't much time."

"It's all the time you need, Paxton. It's all the time you've got."

There came the grim finality of a disconnecting click.

I hung up. Cold sweat formed on my forehead and under my armpits as I walked across the apartment to a locked closet. I unlocked the door, and the sight of Barbara's dresses hanging there made my throat go tight with apprehension because I couldn't fight back. There were her street frocks, her negligees, her little slippers. Unless I obeyed orders, she might never wear them again. A faint fragrance drifted to my nostrils. Barbara's fragrance, clinging daintily to her dresses.

"God . . . !" I whispered.

I knew what I had to do. I pulled down a flat leather packet off the upper shelf and lifted a .32 automatic from my other suit. I crossed over to the bureau, took a handkerchief from the top drawer and scissored two eye-holes in it. I thrust the handkerchief and the gun into my coat pocket, poked the flat leather packet under my shirt. Then I put on my hat and left the apartment, went down to my coupé parked at the curb.

I drove hell-for-leather toward Glendale Airport.

Distance and traffic signals cost me fifteen precious minutes. But I finally got there. I skirted the field to its far side, stopped a little way beyond the private hangar marked Heinrich Kunkel Aero Co. That was where Todd Leland and I had toiled elbow to elbow for six long, weary months. I peered through the gloom. The hangar was dark. It looked deserted.

Ten more minutes later, a light winked on inside the hangar office at the rear of the structure. I saw Todd Leland's profile silhouetted against the dirt-streaked window. That was what I had been waiting for.

I adjusted the handkerchief mask over my face, drew my automatic and stole forward.

My palm was clammy-cold against the gun's matching coldness. The night itself was no blacker than the shadows that were on my heart as I stealthily approached the building before me. For half a year, Todd Leland and I had worked to perfect that bombing-plane control device for the War Department, Todd laboring on the radio part of it while I did the mechanical aeronautics end. Now the job was finished — and I was turning Judas. I was going to doublecross my partner; I was going to sell my country down the river.

It wasn't nice to think about it. I tried not to think about it. I tried to keep my mind on Barbara, whose life was at stake.

The office looked bare and denuded as I softly opened the door. I missed my draughting tables littered with blueprints, the workbenches cluttered with Todd Leland's wires and condensers and experimental radio apparatus. Impotent anger welled through me when I thought of all the work we'd done, work that now would go to benefit some foreign power.

Todd didn't hear me come in. He was busy opening the office safe. His suitcase was on the floor nearby, packed; he was all set to catch the midnight sleeper plane for Washington. Over across the field, the sleek DC-4 airliner was already being tractored out onto the concrete runway.

One final quarter-turn of the dial, and Todd swung the door of the safe outward. He reached in, brought forth a flat leather packet that duplicated the one inside my shirt. He straightened up.

I jammed my automatic against the base of his spine.

"I'll take that," I said and snatched the packet out of his grasp.

He turned around, slowly. "Damn you —" he started to yell.

"Quiet," I warned him. I disguised my voice as much as I could.

He glared at me, his eyes trying to probe through the mask I was wearing. Then, abruptly, his lips twisted in a sardonic grin.

"You're not so smart, mister," he growled.

I didn't answer him. I backed toward the door.

"Those plans won't do you any good," he said. "They aren't worth a damn without the other half. And the other half are where you'll never lay your lousy hands on them."

"What makes you think so?" I sparred, still backing away and keeping him covered.

"My partner has them," he snapped at me. "Do you think Nick Paxton and I would be saps enough to keep the specifications all in one place? Like hell! You damned foreign agents approached us too many times, offered us too many bribes. Nick and I made sure nothing like this would be pulled on us. Not successfully, I mean."

I said: "You talk too much," and reached around behind me for the doorknob.

Todd kept right on trying to sell me on the futility of the hold-up.

"I'm taking my half of the plans to Washington tonight. Nick Paxton is to follow me in a day or so with his half. We arranged it that way, so that in case either of us got hijacked, the hijackers would draw blank. Better hand back that packet, friend. It's worthless to your government without Nick Paxton's blueprints."

"So you think," I said, and stabbed my thumb at the light switch.

Todd did the unexpected. He hurled himself at me before I could jab the office dark. He came with both fists swinging. He was like a maniac.

I let him have it. I had to, even though I hated myself for doing it. I clipped him across the temple with the muzzle end of my automatic. Not too hard; I didn't want to hurt him. After all, he was my friend.

His eyes went glassy. He sagged. And as he went down, he clawed out with his left hand as if to support himself. His outstretched fingers raked my face, caught in the mask. The mask was ripped away, Todd stared at me, stupidly.

"Nick! Nick Paxton!" he exclaimed.

Then he hit the floor, unconscious.

That was bad. Now I was in for it, I knew. I had hoped to pull the stick-up without Todd Leland recognizing me. Then he would never have known my part in the deal. But my luck was out. Once Todd regained consciousness he would go to the police, make a full report. A dragnet would be spread for me.

WELL, it couldn't be helped now. Maybe I could reach the Border, escape into Mexico before the law caught up with me. Barbara and I could start life all over again in one of the banana republics, perhaps. When I thought of Barbara, my nerves tightened. I had to find her, save her — and I had to do it before midnight. That gave me exactly thirty minutes. My wrist-watch showed half-past eleven as I snapped off the office light and scuttled out into the hangar proper.

Thirty minutes in which to reach that hotel over in Burbank! It would be touch-and-go. I cursed whatever foreign operatives had put me in this spot. Then I froze.

Somebody was coming into the hangar from the front.

I didn't have a chance to hide. The big overhead incandescents blazed into raw white life. I blinked, stared ahead. I saw Gus Kunkel and Kunkel's little swarthy-skinned chauffeur, Steve Wallack, coming toward me. I'd often wondered why, with so many Americans out of work, Kunkel didn't hire somebody without a European twist in his tongue to drive his big car. Wallack's face was bland, impassive; his narrow eyes expressionless. Kunkel looked surprised to see me.

Kunkel owned the hangar. He was the one who had put up the money to finance the Leland-Paxton experiments. He was a pudgy, Americanized European who liked to boast of his patriotism, his love of his adopted country.

"Nick Paxton!" he said. "What the devil are you doing here?"

"Seeing Todd Leland off," I lied.

"Has he gone?"

I nodded, fighting not to show my uneasiness. "He went over to the plane five or ten minutes ago," I said. If Kunkel went into the office and discovered Todd Leland lying senseless there, I was sunk. Why the hell was he staring at me so queerly?

"I wanted to tell him good-by and wish him luck," he said. "I think I'll walk across the field and catch him." He turned to Wallack. "You drive the car around and meet me at the administration building."

Wallack nodded and went out.

"Coming with me, Paxton?" Kunkel asked.

I was desperate to get away. "No, thanks," I said. "My car's outside. I've got some errands to do."

My heart drummed against my ribs as I watched Kunkel leave the hangar. Time was leaking away, time I couldn't afford to lose. My lips were dry as I heard the receding purr of Kunkel's limousine heading for the road that circled the field. I listened to the fading footfalls of Kunkel himself as he strode across the hard, oiled surface of the runway. Then I pelted into the night, hurled myself into my coupé. I kicked the starter, headed desperately for Burbank.

It was five minutes before twelve when I skidded to a halt in front of the third-rate Norcross Hotel. I ran into the lobby, crossed it without even a glance at the desk clerk and took the stairs two at a clip. I reached a door marked 210 and knocked.

THERE was a radio playing in the room, tuned in on a swing-band. My nerves were so taut that the sound of the switch being snapped off was like the report of a gun. Then a woman's voice seeped through the thin panel. It was throaty, softly guttural.

"Who is there?" it asked.

"Nick Paxton," I said.

The door opened. I stared into the cold blue eyes of the woman who had questioned me. Her hair was the color of wheat-straw, her complexion like cream and roses, her dress too tight on her curves. She had an automatic in her right hand. I got the impression that her slim fingers weren't strangers to the feel of a trigger.

"Come in, Mr. Paxton," she drawled.

I walked in. She closed the door. Then she searched me, lifted my gun. "A dangerous toy, Mr. Paxton," she purred.

"Where's Barbara?" I demanded. "Where's my wife?"

"Safe enough. Did you bring what you were told to bring?"

I tossed both leather envelope-cases on the table. They seemed of little importance now, yet the information they contained might sway the fate of nations. I wasn't interested in that. I wanted my wife. I said so.

"Really, Mr. Paxton," the blond woman smiled. "Do you think we'd be so stupid as to have her here?"

When I stopped to think about it, I could see what she was driving at. She and her confederates weren't too sure I'd show up with the plans. I might have risked calling the police.

Her gun still menaced me. "I'll look at the plans to be certain. Then I'll telephone and arrange for your wife's release. The phone is in the next room. Meantime —" From a drawer of the small table which held the tiny portable radio, she took a pair of handcuffs. She wasn't taking any chances on me.

Warned by her automatic, I stood still while she snapped one of the cuffs on my left wrist and looped the other bracelet around a steam-pipe in the far corner. If it hadn't been for Barbara's danger, I'd have fought through hell for those plans. But I didn't dare fight, the way things stood.

The woman made a hasty examination of the specifications in the two packets. She seemed satisfied. She laid them on the table beside the radio, beyond my reach, and went into the next room.

A scheme popped into my head. I might not hear what was said over the phone, but if I could get hold of the little radio and turn it on, maybe I'd be able to count the dial-clicks and figure out the number being called. Then, if the blonde and her pals tried to doublecross me, I'd have something to go on.

I couldn't reach the table. So I slid the handcuff down the steam-pipe to the floor, stretched myself out on my back and fished my feet toward the table-leg. I made contact; rocked the table. It didn't quite tip over, but the radio slid off and I caught it between my ankles. I pulled it to me, flipped the switch.

The loud-speaker hummed into life just as the blonde woman began dialing in the room next door. I counted the dialing clicks. One, four, two, four, four, nine, one. From the other room I could hear the low blur of the woman's voice:

"This is Frieda. He brought them. Better tell —" She dropped her tone and I couldn't get what she said after that.

There was something damned familiar about the phone number she had dialed. I translated it in my mind. The first "one" would be

"ABC." The second "four" represented "GHI" — and in that area, it could only mean the local exchange, which was Citrus. Therefore, the number she was talking to was Citrus 2-4491.

I'd called it many a time, myself. It was Gus Kunkel's residence!

RAGE choked me. So Kunkel was the man behind the kidnaping of my wife! He had financed Todd Leland and me until we'd perfected our invention. Now he wanted to get it away from us without revealing his own identity in the matter — so he could make a fortune by peddling the device to his original fatherland! All his talk about American patriotism was so much bunk!

I was balancing the tiny radio in my hand as I heard the woman returning. I was squatting on my haunches now, my left hand still cuffed to the steam-pipe. If I could throw the little receiving-set straight enough —

I jerked its connecting cord out of the plug. And as the Frieda female came through the door, I let her have it. The radio weighed about five pounds, and it clipped her a glancing blow on the chin. She went to her knees. Then she toppled on her face. She was out, cold.

But my predicament was just as bad as ever. I had seen her drop the handcuff key inside the low-slashed vee of her dress, and when she fell, she was still on the other side of the room — a good six feet past my reach. There I was, cuffed to the pipe, the key in the woman's bosom, and the plans in plain sight — but as inaccessible to me as if they'd been fifty miles away.

I lived ten years in the next two minutes. Then I cursed my own stupidity for not seeing a way out. The woman was beginning to stir. In another moment or so she'd regain consciousness. If she happened to be sore enough to use her gun, I was washed up. I had to act fast.

There was a nine-by-twelve rug on the floor. If I just had strength enough in my one arm to grasp the rug's edge and slide it toward me with the weight of the woman's body, the weight of the furniture, perhaps.

I grabbed the rug and pulled it. Slowly the woman came toward me, head-first. If I could get that key, it meant freedom for me — and for Barbara. I'd be able to save the plans, too. And Gus Kunkel would never again have occasion to proclaim his allegiance to the United States. I loved the ground he was going to be planted in.

At last I tugged the rug enough to bring the woman close to me. I ripped her dress open all the way to the waist It was no time for niceties.

I wanted that key. I got it.

A minute later I was loose, the precious plans were under my shirt and the blonde was handcuffed to the steam-pipe that had been my own hitching-post. I taped her mouth with some adhesive I found in the bathroom. Then I threw the key out the window.

GUS KUNKEL lived in a big house on the top of a hill near where Glendale cuts into East Hollywood. How I got there without being arrested, I'll never know. I certainly broke all the traffic laws ever written. And I wasn't taking any more chances with the plans.

My coupé was an Oldie with a drip-pan under the motor. When I stopped in front of Kunkel's driveway, I took an oilproof slicker I had in the back of the car and ripped a square piece out of it. I wrapped the two leather packets in the oiled square of cloth, opened the hood and slid the little bundle under my engine.

While I was doing it, a taxicab came roaring up the hill. I crouched down behind some bushes as the cab skidded into the driveway and stopped. The corrugated grip of the automatic I'd got back from the blonde felt good to my palm. I watched.

I saw the taxi's door swing open under the porte-cochere of Kunkel's house. Kunkel himself tumbled out of the cab and tossed the hacker a bill. The cab pulled away as Kunkel made for his front door.

I raced across the lawn, my feet making no sound on the thick turf. The first warning Kunkel had of my presence was the pressure of my gun against his back.

"One bleat out of you and they'll send your ashes to the Fatherland in a vase," I told him.

He trembled. I could feel the shiver coursing through him. As he always did when excited, he lapsed into broken English.

"Dis iss a hold-up, ja? Mine money iss in der hip pocket. You take heem and —"

"I don't want your stinking dough," I snarled. "I want my wife."

With his hands high, he turned around. "Nick!" he gasped. If his surprise was feigned, the movies had lost another star when Kunkel went into the aviation business. "Nick Paxton — haff you gone grazy? Vot do I know about your wife?"

"You had her kidnaped to force me into turning the Paxton-Leland plans over to you. Don't stall. You're washed up, Kunkel. I did give the plans to your blond lady friend, so that she'd phone you an okay to turn

Barbara loose. But later I conked the blonde and got the specifications back — and I tracked you down at the same time. Now I'm calling the plays."

He seemed dazed. "I don't know vot you're talking about, Nick. I thought Todd Leland vent east vith his half of the plans at midnight. The plane took off joost as I got across the field. I vaited for Wallack to come vith mine limousine, but he didn't show up. I took a taxi and came home —"

"Wallack!" I whispered. "Maybe he's the one the dame Frieda telephoned, here at your house!" Not that I believe Kunkel to be in the clear. But it was possible that he and his chauffeur were working together. I said: "Come on, Kunkel. You and I are going to find Wallack. Keep your hands where I can see them. Walk ahead of me."

He seemed willing enough. Almost too willing. Once he and the chauffeur got together, the odds would be two to one against me. But that was a risk I'd have to accept. At least I had the advantage of surprise on my side.

I prodded Kunkel toward the garage, saw Kunkel's limousine there. So that much of my guess was correct; Wallack had come straight home — probably in order to accept the blond woman's call. There was a light in the living quarters above the garage; the chauffeur must be up there now, I figured. I forced Kunkel up the stairs ahead of me until we reached the door of Wallack's room. I knocked.

"Is that you, Frieda?" Wallack's voice asked.

I stiffened. Frieda was the blonde's name. I pitched my tone to a purring falsetto. "Yes. Let me in."

The door opened. I shoved Kunkel in front of me as a shield. I covered Wallack with my automatic and said: "Reach, rat."

Wallack went pasty. His mouth opened, but no words came out.

"Talk fast, Wallack!" I said. "Where's my wife?"

He seemed to read the determination in my eyes, must have realized I'd kill him unless he gave me straight answers. In his precise English with its foreign-flavored accent he said:

"I do not know where she is."

"You lie!" I blazed.

"The kidnaping of Mrs. Paxton was not a part of my plan," he insisted desperately. "When Frieda telephoned me and told me you had delivered the specifications to her, I had no further interest in your wife. You cannot hold me responsible. I only agreed to buy the Paxton-

Leland invention; I did not care how it was obtained."

"So you agreed to buy the invention!" I snarled. I knew that no such agreement had been made with me. "Was it Kunkel?"

"No. It was —"

From the doorway behind me a voice spoke.

"All right, Wallack. You needn't mention my name. I'm afraid it's already been guessed. Drop your gun, Nick. I'm sorry, but I've got you covered."

Todd Leland's voice!

I dropped my gun, half-turned to face him. He stood at the threshold with a .38 Colt in his steady fist and a bandage over his head where I'd clipped him, back at the hangar office. A wry grimace twisted his lips.

"I guess you think I'm a louse, Nick," he said. "Maybe I am. But I needed money badly — and quickly. My kid brother is in a jam at the bank where he works. A bad jam. And Wallack offered me a hundred thousand, spot cash —"

"But, Todd," I blurted, "this doesn't make sense! I stole the plans from you!"

"That's the way I juggled it, Nick. I realized you'd never go for a cash sell-out, and I knew my half of the plans were worthless without yours. So I had to figure some way of getting your half without you suspecting me; I wanted to make you think that you yourself were the guilty one."

"God!" I whispered.

"We may as well be truthful, now that you know this much," he went on. "I knew your most vulnerable spot would be Barbara. So I had my brother kidnap her and phone you. I knew you'd steal my half of the plans and then take both halves to Wallack's woman at the Norcross Hotel. That's why I allowed you to conk me. And by putting on that act of recognizing you when I tore your mask away, I had you in a spot where you'd never be able to bleat."

Dumbly I just stared at him. He went on: "Just now, I came here for my pay-off. I heard enough to let me know you'd smeared the deal —"

"I smeared it plenty," I breathed, still hardly believing that my own partner had engineered the whole thing. Wallack and Kunkel stood beyond me, all of us covered by Todd's gun. It was like a nightmare.

Todd's eyes looked desperate. "You've got to understand, Nick," he said, "I don't like this any more than you do. But my brother needs that money and I'm in too deep to back out, now. After all, Wallack is acting for a friendly power. The invention will never be used against this country. I want those plans, Nick. I mean to have them. Where are they?"

"Where's Barbara?" I countered.

"She'll be released when I give the word. I won't give the word until I get those plans and turn them over to Wallack — for cash. You can't stop me now, Nick."

I don't know what made me say it. Certainly it wasn't because I feared for Barbara's safety, I knew Todd's brother wouldn't harm her, if it came right down to cases. Whatever happened, she would be okay. But when I saw the hysteria in Todd Leland's eyes, I spoke.

"The plans are in my car," I muttered. After all, half of the invention belonged to Todd. And maybe I could still talk him out of selling them. "They're in my car," I repeated, "but you don't want to —"

That was as far as I got. Todd should have known better. Keeping three men covered is no cinch. Wallack had been watching for his chance, and now he whipped a Luger from under his chauffeur's uniform-coat. He cut loose with it.

His first shot smashed Todd's gun out of his hand. "Now the plans are mine — without payment! You will all die, in the name of Der Fuehrer!" He fired again, and Todd doubled over, a bullet through his mid-riff.

I braced myself for the impact of a death slug. Gus Kunkel almost collapsed. Wallack triggered again, but nothing happened. The Luger had jammed.

He cursed gutturally and dived for the doorway. I tried to stop him. His fist caught me on the chin. I staggered. He got by me and went clattering down the steps. I could hear his heels hammering on the driveway as he raced to the street where my coupé was parked.

Todd Leland straightened up. Blood was spreading across the front of his shirt, and his right hand was bullet-creased. But with all that, he beat me to the door. "So Wallack was working for the Nazis!" he gasped. And he plunged down the stairs.

I went after him. But he was already behind the wheel of Gus Kunkel's big limousine. It roared away before I could leap for the running-board.

Out at the curb, I heard my own coupé surging into the night with Wallack driving it. Wallack was making his getaway with the plans —

and Todd Leland, wounded, was pursuing him!

I heard Kunkel descending. "Have you got another car?" I yelled.

"My daughter's Ford. In the garage, Nick."

I found it, piled in. Kunkel jammed himself alongside me as I gunned the V-eight backward to the driveway. I hit the street in second, and started after Todd. In a hundred yards I had the speedometer up to forty, then fifty.

Remembering the down-grade, I eased off for the turn at the foot of the hill. There wasn't too much speed in my coupé, which Wallack was driving; and Todd Leland, in the Kunkel limousine, was making knots. But the coupé was shorter and could make the turns faster. It was anybody's race. I was gaining on Todd, but he wasn't gaining on Wallack.

There was a hairpin turn at the foot of the hill. At the speed Todd was driving that big car, I didn't think he could make it. Then I caught my breath. He didn't even try to make the turn. There was a low embankment just this side of the spot where the road doubled back on itself. Todd deliberately wheeled the limousine over the edge. In a flash, I understood his plan. If the limousine held together, it would slam across the intervening space and come out on the lower section of the road, straight in Wallack's path as he came around the curve.

In the uncertain light I saw the big car go jouncing across the rough rocks, tires bursting with every turn of the wheels. It lurched across the flat place at the bottom of the embankment and landed squarely in Wallack's path. The Nazi agent tried to slow up, but the brakes on my coupé were none too good. With Wallack screaming at the wheel, my little jalopy whammed into the limousine's side. The crunching crash of metal could be heard for blocks. Wallack's shriek died suddenly as his head smashed forward into the windshield and shattered the glass. Razor-sharp shards sliced through his gullet. . . .

I stood on the V-eight's brakes, scrambled out, with Kunkel scurrying after me. We stumbled down the embankment on foot.

"Todd!" I yelled as I saw him come weaving out of the big limousine. I caught the flicker of flame licking the two twisted wrecks. "The plans — under the motor of my coupé —" Then I cursed as a turning rock twisted myankle and sent me sprawling.

Below me, fire roared as it caught the spilled gasoline. Yellow tongues hissed skyward. I saw Todd Leland approaching the heart of the blaze. I knew what he was going to do. I could almost hear the frying of flesh as he reached into that flaming hell and raised my coupé's hood.

I couldn't have stopped him. Nobody could have stopped him. Flame cloaked his form for a moment, like a white-hot shroud. Gus Kunkel was whispering: "God! God in Heaven!" Then Todd Leland came staggering away from the wreckage. He had something in his arms. It was the square of slicker-wrapped plans.

He collapsed in the middle of the road as I reached him. His face was a blotch of scorched, blackened flesh. I beat at the smoking shreds of his clothing with my bare hands. I bent over him.

"Wallack's dead," he whispered through pain-twisted lips. "But here . . . are the...plans. . . . Listen, Nick . . . I wouldn't have . . . done it . . . if I'd known . . . Wallack was . . . a Nazi. . . ."

"Take it easy, Todd," I said gently. "I'll get a doctor. I'll —"

"No good," he moaned. "I'm . . . done for. . . . Tell my brother . . . to take his . . . medicine . . . like a man. . . ."

"I'll tell him, Todd. Maybe I can help him. I'll try."

"Thanks, Nick . . . you'll find Barbara . . . at the kid's apartment . . . don't hang a . . . kidnap rap . . . on him . . . don't let . . . the world . . . know . . . I . . . almost sold . . . out . . . my country. . . ."

He grew quiet. Deathly quiet. I said a little prayer for his soul. He'd made a mistake, but had rectified it.

Gus Kunkel touched my arm. "Nobody need ever know the truth, Nick," he said softly. "We'll tell the police I was coming home in my limousine and there was a collision. And I'll put up the money to get Todd's brother out of trouble. Maybe you'd better go, now. Go find Barbara."

I went back up the hill to the V-eight. I found Barbara at Todd's brother's apartment.

"Nick . . . oh, my dear!" she cried brokenly. I took her in my arms.

MURDER'S MESSENGER

The yellow-haired man walked into my private office. He looked worried.

He said: "Are you Dan Turner, the private detective?"

I said: "Yes. What can I do for you?"

He sat down. He hauled five crisp new centuries from his billfold and tossed them on my desk in front of me. Then he said: "Can you prevent murder, Mr. Turner?"

I looked at him. I've been a private dick in Hollywood for a hell of a long time. But this was the first time anybody had ever asked me if I knew how to stop a murder from happening. I set fire to a cigarette to cover my surprise. Then I said: "Just what do you mean?"

He said: "Permit me to introduce myself, Mr. Turner. I am Konrad Vincennes. I am with Altamount Studios." There was no trace of accent to his words; but I noticed a certain precise orthodoxy of speech, a careful choosing of sentences indicating that to him English was a foreign tongue.

And the minute he mentioned his name, I tabbed him. He was a Rumanian tenor, and Altamount had imported him to star in musicals. He was a good-looking bird — lots of sex-appeal. The kind that spinsters and parlor-maids always fall for. He'd been in Hollywood about a month, and the papers had played him up big.

"A certain young woman of my acquaintance has been threatened with death," he went on. "I want you to protect her. Her name is Ysobel LeSage."

I said: "For God's sake!" Because I knew Ysobel LeSage. At least, I knew her by reputation. She was a foreign star, too. She worked for N-D-N Productions. A swell-looker, and I don't mean maybe. Lots of hips and breasts and legs, if you get my meaning. She had what it took to make the men fall for her — and it was rumored that half the big shots of Hollywood shared her favors . . .

I said: "Who's doing the threatening?"

Vincennes darted a swift look about my office, as thought to make sure he wasn't being overheard. Then he lowered his voice to a semi-whisper and said: "The threat was an anonymous one. But I have reason to believe that it came from a man who occupies a high position here in

Hollywood. Yet I have no proof; and therefore I cannot go to the police with only my suspicions."

"A Hollywood big shot, eh?" I said, "What's his name?"

"John Sixtus, production manager of N-D-N Pictures!" the yellow-haired man answered.

I hid my incredulity behind a cloud of gasper smoke. "John Sixtus?" I said slowly. "Why the hell should John Sixtus desire the death of Ysobel LeSage?"

Vincennes said: "He is jealous of her." Then he picked up those five crisp centuries from my desk and handed them to me. "This is your retainer, Mr. Turner, if you will accept the case."

I said: "Just what would you expect me to do?"

"You are to protect Ysobel LeSage at all costs!" he flung back at me, desperately.

I thought it over. I've never played bodyguard to anybody. It's out of my line. But this Ysobel LeSage chicken — well, she was a knockout; and I might have a chance to find out how nice she really was, if I took the job of being her guardian angel . . .

I said: "All right, Vincennes. I'll go have a talk with Miss LeSage. Where does she live?"

Vincennes gave me an address in Beverly Hills. He said: "She will be home inside an hour. You will go to her then?"

I looked at my watch. It was a little after four in the afternoon. I'd just have time to go home, shower, shave, and down a couple of hookers of Scotch. I said: "Okay. You've hired a detective."

The yellow-haired Vincennes looked at me gratefully. "Thank you!" he whispered. "Perhaps I shall see you at Miss LeSage's house a little later."

I saw him to the door. Then I put on my hat, closed my office and went home.

I shaved close to the skin. No use roughing up Ysobel LeSage's complexion, in case I got to kiss her . . . ! I showered and killed off about a third of a bottle of Vat 69. Then I climbed into my jalopy and headed for Beverly Hills.

While I drove, I wondered just how much truth there might be in Konrad Vincennes' suspicions of John Sixtus, the production chief of N-D-N Studios. Personally, I didn't take a hell of a lot of stock in it. Sixtus was too big a figure in Hollywood to be involved in a murder-threat plot. He was too smart — too old a hand. The whole thing sounded fantastic as the devil. But on the other hand, Konrad Vincennes, the Rumanian tenor, had slipped me five hundred clams — and there was nothing fantastic about that! I had the geetus in my pocket!

Dusk was commencing to fall when I got within a block of Ysobel LeSage's address. Even if the air hadn't been balmy, I'd have known it was springtime; because I was subconsciously aware of asthmatic harmonies emanating from a hand-organ at the far intersection. Grindorgans always show up in Hollywood in April.

Then, over the hand-organ's wheezing melody, I heard an abrupt sound — a sharp report. It might have been an automobile's backfire . . . or the bark of a small-caliber pistol. I stiffened. I drew in to the curb.

For in single instant I stared ahead into the twilight. Through the gathering gloom I saw a front door open in a house at the very end of the block. A tall, slender man emerged. He peered, first to the right and then to the left. Then he stepped off the porch to the pavement. He headed for the car corner. Some inner hunch whispered in my ear. And I always follow my hunches. I opened the door of my coupe, got out, strode forward.

I saw the organ-grinder blocking the tall, slender man's path. The organ-grinder's oversized monkey, tethered to the end of a long leather cord, leaped chattering to its master's shoulder. The organ-grinder extended his battered hat toward the slender, tall man who was trying to go around him.

Then the tall man hesitated. His hand plunged into his pocket, emerged with a coin. He flung it into the extended hat; and then roughly, irritably, he shoved the hand-organ man aside and almost ran around the corner, out of sight.

I leaped ahead. I smelled something fishy. I gained the front door of the house from which the tall man had come. Its front door was still open. I took a gander at the numerals over the door. I frowned. It was the address which had been given me by Konrad Vincennes. It was the house where Ysobel LeSage lived!

I whirled toward the organ-grinder.

Then I said: "What the hell — !"

The hand-organ man and his monkey had vanished while I was standing there staring at the address over the open door!

I turned and took the stone steps of the house in two jumps. Something was wrong somewhere — I sensed it. I dashed inside, through the open front door.

I raised my voice. "Miss LeSage!" I called out.

There was no answer.

There was a living room to my right as I stood there in the rapidly-darkening hallway. I pivoted on my heel and plunged into the room.

I felt the skin tighten at the nape of my neck.

In the fading light that filtered in through the open front window, I saw a sprawled form on the carpet at my feet. The body of a woman!

She lay face-upward. Her features held a hard, worldly beauty marred only by the pain-contorted twist of her rouged lips and the lifeless stare of her open, glazing eyes. And I recognized her from pictures I'd seen of her.

She was Ysobel LeSage, the wren I'd been hired to guard!

She'd been clad in nothing but a thin negligee. In falling, the robe had fallen open. I could see her naked hips and thighs and legs. I could see the buxom mounds of her breasts; and I knew then why so many men had fallen for her.

I dropped to one knee, breathing hard. I pushed away the coal-black masses of hair from Ysobel LeSage's white forehead. There was a round blue hole in her left temple. Blood oozed from it, and brains too.

I grabbed her limp wrist. There was no flutter of pulse. I put my palm beneath her left breast. Her heart had stopped beating. Ysobel LeSage was as dead as a herring.

I got to my feet, and my right hand felt wet, sticky. I looked at it. My fingers were all bloody, where I'd pushed the girl's black hair back from her forehead. . . .

I flicked out a handkerchief, carefully wiped my mitt free of blood. Then I looked around me. Something glittered on the carpet, in the waning daylight.

It was a tiny roscoe — a small-caliber revolver.

Once more I yanked out my handkerchief. Very carefully I dropped it over the gun, so I wouldn't disturb any possible fingerprints. Then I picked up the gat, sniffed it's muzzle. That rod had been recently fired!

I looked at it. And then, abruptly, a voice from the living room doorway said: "Stand where you are! Don't make a move!"

I froze in my tracks. Then I chanced a swift gander — and I found myself staring into the hard eyes of a uniformed copper who had a service .38 in his fist. He was pointing the .38 at my gizzard.

"What's the idea, fella?" I barked at him.

He said: "You wouldn't know, would you, wise guy?" Then his eyes flickered toward the almost-naked corpse of Ysobel LeSage, on the floor. He looked at me again, sneering. "You wouldn't know anything about this dead dame, I don't suppose? And you were wiping your fingerprints off that roscoe just to pass the time away!"

I said: "See here, copper —"

He grinned at me, sardonically. "Damned lucky thing I happened to be cruising past here in my radio car when I got the flash from headquarters! Three minutes later and you'd have made your get-away!"

I narrowed my eyes. "Somebody phoned headquarters?" I asked.

"Yeah. Unfortunately for you, someone heard a shot. Heard you bumping off this dame here. Come on now, buddy — hand me that rod!"

I said: *"Catch!"* Then I threw the handkerchief-covered roscoe full at his kisser.

The cop's hands went up automatically. That's what I'd been waiting for. Now I sprang forward. My shoulder crashed into the bull's chest, and he went backward, off-balance.

While he was still staggering, I swung on him. I brought one up from my knees and let that copper have it right on the button. I hated to do it; but I was in a tough spot. There was no other way out.

My knuckles took him on the point of the jaw like a charge of dynamite. The harness-bull sagged like an emptied sack.

I leaped over him, I knew he was out; knew he wouldn't try to plug me in the back. When I paste a guy, he stays pasted for quite a while! I flung myself out of that living room, into the hallway.

I catapulted full-tilt into a man who was just entering through the front door.

I staggered, righted myself. My hand dived for the .32 automatic I always carry strapped under my armpit, in a shoulder-holster. My rod came out. And then I lowered it. I recognized the man I'd bumped into.

It was the yellow-haired Konrad Vincennes, the Rumanian tenor who had hired me to guard Ysobel LeSage!

I said: "For God's sake! Where the hell did you come from — and how long have you been here?"

Vincennes stared at me as though he'd been slapped in the mush by a ghost. He said: "I — I just drove up here to see Ysobel — to ask her if you'd been here to talk to her. Is — is anything wrong?"

I said: "Is anything wrong?" Then I grabbed him, hauled him

toward the living room. It was dark now. I wrenched out my pocket torch, swept its circle of blue-white light over the floor, rested it for a brief instant on Ysobel LeSage's lovely, lifeless corpse.

Konrad Vincennes cried out in a stunned voice. "It — it is Ysobel — Ysobel LeSage! Oh, God . . . !" He darted past me, threw himself toward the girl's undraped body.

My arms streaked out and pinioned him. "You damn' fool!" I grated. "She's dead. You can't do her any good now!" Then I pulled him into the hallway. "We've got to get out of here!" I told him.

"But — but why?"

"There's a cop over there in the corner of the room!" I answered. "I bashed him silly. Had to. He was putting the pinch on me for murdering the LeSage girl. Let's go before he wakes up and drags us both to the clink!" I yanked the Rumanian tenor to the front door, pushed him out of the house, followed him.

"Where's your car?" I asked him.

"I — I came in a taxi."

"Then we'll go in mine — together!" I said. I piloted Vincennes past the parked radio car in which that uniformed copper had arrived. We reached my own coupe, piled into it. I kicked the starter. We went away from there — fast.

After a while, Vincennes said: "Where are you going?"

I said: "The Hollywood *Herald* building."

"I — I don't understand," he whispered.

I said: "That uniformed shamus didn't recognize me. I'm safe enough for the present; I'm not likely to be pinched. But in the meantime I've got work to do. I've got to find out who killed Ysobel LeSage — unless I want to face a murder-rap myself!"

I flipped my hack past a red light and headed for town. Konrad Vincennes said: "I know who killed Ysobel! It was John Sixtus!"

I said: "Maybe so. But I won't know for sure until I can find a certain guy and ask him some questions."

"What do you mean?" Vincennes said.

"I saw a tall bozo running out of Ysobel LeSage's house just after that shot was fired," I answered. "And John Sixtus is a tall bozo."

"You saw his face?" the yellow-haired tenor asked me tautly.

I said: "No, dammit. But there's someone who did see him!"

"Who?"

"An organ-grinder who was playing just outside Ysobel's door. The tall bozo bumped into him, gave him a coin. So now I'm going to get a newspaper picture of John Sixtus. Then I'm going to hunt up every organ-grinder in Hollywood. There can't be over three or four — they're a dying breed. But I've got to locate the one who was playing outside Ysobel' LeSage's house. I've got to show him a picture of John Sixtus.

"If he recognizes it as the man who came running out of Ysobel's door after that shot was fired, we'll have Sixtus where the hair is short!"

Vincennes said: "Then you've got to find that organ-grinder! You must!"

"Yeah," I answered grimly. "Moreover, that grind-organ man is the only alibi I've got for my own self. He's the only one who saw me come up to the LeSage house *after* that shot was fired!"

Just then I parked before the office of the Hollywood *Herald*. I got out of my hack and said: "You scram now, Vincennes. And keep your face buttoned. I'll get in touch with you if I need you."

He took it on the lam down the street. Then I went inside the newspaper building; went upstairs to the editorial department. I went back to the file-room — the "morgue", as the newspaper boys call it.

A girl clerk came toward me. She was young, and she had tawny hair, and she had a carload of "it." She wore a tailored skirt that outlined her nice, slender hips; and her mannish silk blouse disclosed the outlines of tender young breasts, firm and solid. She smiled at me interrogatively.

I grinned back and said: "Have you got a good full-face picture of John Sixtus, the N-D-N executive, baby?"

For an instant she seemed a little startled — or at least I got that impression. Then her long lashes masked her eyes. "We probably have," she answered me. Then she went to a cabinet and riffled through its contents. She came back to me, handed me a newspaper photo — a picture of John Sixtus, tall, thin, commanding. She said: "Is this what you mean?"

I said: "Yeah. May I have it?"

The girl frowned. "I'm sorry, but it's against the rules to loan pictures from our files."

I looked around. There was nobody else in the little file-room. I pulled a ten-spot out of my jeans and waved it. I said: "Will this change your mind, honey?"

"No," she answered quietly. "It won't."

Then I grinned at her and slipped an arm around her waist. I managed to touch one of her breasts, through her blouse. It felt nice and warm and firm. I couldn't find any trace of brassiere under the thin silk . . .

The girl drew a sharp breath. She made a half-hearted gesture to push me away. But that was evidently just for the sake of appearances; because when I persisted, she let

me have my way. I managed to unfasten the front of her blouse and explore a bit . . . It was damned nice exploring, too. . . .

After a while I said: "I'm Dan Turner, private dick. Maybe you've heard of me?"

She looked at me dreamily, "Yes. I've heard of you," she whispered.

I said: "Listen, darling. I need that picture of John Sixtus. A dame has been bumped off, and I think Sixtus did it. You let me have that picture, and I'll see that you won't regret it. Maybe we can throw a party somewhere, after I've nailed John Sixtus."

So she gave me the picture. "You'll bring it back when you've finished with it?" she whispered.

I said: "You bet. Wild horses couldn't keep me away from you, baby. And the picture will give me an excuse to see you again!" Then I went out.

I got into my jalopy and drove to the Italian quarter of Los Angeles. I went into a little Dago grocery store. I made some inquiries. I found out that there were only three known organ-grinders left in town — last remnants of a vanishing guild. I had their names and addresses, I climbed back into my coupe and started for the first one.

That call was a disappointment. So was my second try, for that matter. The first organ-grinder proved to be a one-legged hunchback. The second one was short, fat, squat. Neither could have been the one I'd seen outside Ysobel LeSage's home at the time of the murder.

So I went to the third and last address on my list.

I rang the bell of a dirty little hovel. A good-looking Italian dame opened the door for me. She was dressed in a sleazy kimono, and she was fairly young. She had coal-black hair and flashing eyes, and her breasts showed through the kimono — lush, buxom, soft, white. I looked at her and said: "Does Giuseppe Palermo live here?"

"What-a you want with him?" the girl demanded.

"I've got to see him — talk to him."

"He's-a not in," she said. But she looked as if she were lying. She looked scared.

So I figured to scare her even more — frighten the truth out of her. I flashed my special-officer badge and said: "Let me in, baby. I've got to find Giuseppe."

I pushed past her, into the house. I walked into a tiny parlor. The Italian dame followed me; looked at me oddly. Then she said: "You wait. I get glass of wine."

She went into a back room. Pretty soon she came back with a beaker of Dago red. I tossed it past my tonsils and sat down on a horse-hair sofa. The Italian baby sat down alongside me and drew a deep sigh. I noticed that she'd allowed her kimono to fall open in front. I took a good look. I saw plenty.

The trouble with me, I can't keep my hands to myself. And besides, that glass of Dago red was creeping through my veins like a fuse; and pretty soon the fuse burned all the way to something that exploded inside me. When that happened, I slipped an arm around the Italian bimbo's waist, under her kimono.

She sighed and nestled close to me. "Kiss-a me!" she hissed hotly.

So I kissed her. And she opened her mouth and tried to swallow me! I've kissed lots of dames in my time, but this Italian baby had more on the ball than I've ever seen. Her arms went around my neck. Her hands were against the back of my head, holding me. She started pressing against me, her buxom breasts against my chest —

I should have known better. I should have sensed something hay-wire. Dames don't usually go that hog-wild so damned quickly. But the possibility of danger never entered my thoughts. I was too busy grabbing; too occupied running my fingers along bare thighs . . . I shoved the girl backward on the sofa. She tipped over plenty easy.

And then I found out why.

All of a sudden she let out a yelp. In Italian she hissed: *"Now get him, Giuseppe!"*

I squirmed sidewise and ducked. I was just in time to get out from under a blackjack. It took me in the shoulder, instead of the noggin. If I hadn't moved at that instant, I'd have met Saint Peter right there and then!

As it was, the blackjack bludgeoned my shoulder and damn' near paralyzed me. In a flash I was on my feet, had dragged out my .32 auto-matic roscoe. I jammed it into the guts of a wild-eyed, bearded bozo who reeked of garlic and who was spitting out a stream of Latin cuss-words.

I said: "Drop that blackjack, you louse!"

The bearded bozo dropped it. Then I looked at him and said: "Are you Giuseppe Palermo?"

"*Si!*" he answered sullenly. Then, in a torrent of words, he said: "You can't deport-a me! Just-a because I lose-a my first-a citizen papers —"

Then I got it. I said: "Oh, for God's sake!" in a disgusted voice. This Giuseppe Palermo had lost his naturalization papers — and he'd thought me to be an immigration officer! That's why his dark-eyed wife had lured me! When she'd gone after that glass of Dago red, she'd planned the whole thing with her hubby. She'd allowed me to play with her — plenty — in order to give Giuseppe a chance to bean me!

But that wasn't what griped me. The thing that got me down was the fact that Giuseppe Palermo wasn't the organ-grinder I was looking for! He had a beard; and the grind-organ man I'd seen playing outside Ysobel LeSage's home at the time of the murder was smooth-shaven!

So I grinned and put away my automatic. I said: "We both made a mistake, Giuseppe. Forget the whole thing!"

"You mean-a I'm not arrest'?"

"Hell, no!" I grunted. And I went out.

I drove back to my apartment in Hollywood. I switched on my living room lights and poured myself a stiff slug of Vat 69. This organ-grinder business had me utsnay. There were supposed to be only three in the entire Los Angeles area, and I'd seen all of them. But none of them was the one I'd seen outside the LeSage residence at the time that murder-shot was fired!

Therefore, there had to be a fourth grind-organ man. And I had to find him. If I didn't, my pants would be in a sling. I needed that missing organ-grinder to prove that I'd been outside Ysobel LeSage's place when the shot was fired!

I tossed down another hooker of the Scotch. And then my front doorbell buzzed.

I yanked the door open. Then I said: "What the hell — !"

There was a man standing there. He was swarthy, poorly-dressed. He had a grind-organ strapped over his shoulder. An over-sized monkey was perched on the organ. The man was the one I'd seen in front of Ysobel LeSage's house!

He took off his battered felt hat and bowed to me. "Pardon, *signor*," he said humbly. "Your name, she's-a Mist' Turner?"

I said: "You're damned right my name's Turner. Come in!"

I dragged him into my living room. Then I said: "Who are you?"

"I am Pietro Conzono, signor. Some friends, they tell-a me you are look for me?"

"You're cockeyed right I was looking for you!" I shot back. "Listen. Were you playing your organ in Beverly Hills this evening around five o'clock?"

He nodded. *"Si, signor."*

I dragged out that picture of John Sixtus, which the tawny-haired Hollywood *Herald* girl had loaned to me. I said: "Take a squint at this, Pietro. Ever see this man before?"

His eyes widened. *"Si, si!"* he bobbed his head. "This-a man, she's-a give me whole silver dollar when he come outa da house!"

I said; "By God, that cinches it! John Sixtus murdered Ysobel LeSage!"

Then a voice from my bedroom doorway said: "John Sixtus didn't kill anybody. Put up your hands — both of you!"

I whirled — and looked into the blazing eyes of the tawny-haired Hollywood *Herald* girl! The blonde baby who'd loaned me that picture of John Sixtus! She had a wicked-looking little nickel-plated rod in her hand, and she was pointing it at my navel.

For a second I was too stunned to think. Then I said: "What the damnation hell are you doing here?"

She said: "I've been hiding in your bedroom since before you came in. I've been waiting for you!"

I said: "How did you know where to find me?"

"You told me your name," she fired back at me evenly.

I said: "Okay. I suppose that explains everything."

She sneered. "You didn't realize that I might be the daughter of John Sixtus, did you? You didn't think a movie executive's daughter might be a cub newspaper girl!" Her eyes narrowed. "Well, if you think you can blackmail my father on a trumped-up murder charge, you're wrong!"

I said: "So that's it!" Then I looked over her shoulder and yelled: "Grab her, Jenkins!"

It was an old gag — old as the hills. If the girl had been more experienced, she might not have fallen for it. As it was, she half-turned toward the bedroom doorway behind her.

That's all I wanted. I leaped for her, grabbed her gun-wrist, twisted.

She struck at me with her free hand; raked my cheek with her finger-nails. She put up quite a struggle. Her silken blouse ripped, exposing her delicious breasts. I wound my arms around her, mashing her bosom flat against my chest. Then, finally, I managed to wrench that vicious little roscoe out of her grasp. I tossed it on the table. Then I took a good look at her.

Lord, she was lovely! The blouse was torn all the way to her naked waist. She was panting, so that her little breasts moved up and down like corks on the ocean. She was like a pagan goddess, and her eyes were blazing fires. I felt like grabbing her right then. . . .

I said: "If you're John Sixtus' daughter, your father killed Ysobel LeSage!"

She went white. "You lie!" she wailed out, "He loved her — wanted to marry her!"

I started to answer; but I didn't get the chance. All of a sudden the front door of my apartment smashed inward with a hell of a crash. Three uniformed cops ploughed into the room — and my friend, Dave Donaldson of the homicide squad, was leading them! Dave's roscoe was out, and he meant business.

I said: "Dave — what the hell — !"

He said: "I always figured you'd make a mistake some day, Turner! You didn't think we'd catch up with you so soon, did you? You forgot that your handkerchief was wrapped around that gun you threw at the cop in Ysobel LeSage's house, just before you popped him silly. We traced you through the laundry mark!"

I said: "Don't be a damned ass, Donaldson. I've got an alibi. It's this Dago organ-grinder here —" And then, even as I said it, the whole truth flashed on me. I knew the answer to the puzzle — knew who'd killed Ysobel LeSage!

But before I could make a move, something happened. There was a flash of brown fur through the air. The organ-grinder's oversized monkey had leaped from the man's shoulder, toward the table. I yelled: "Look out, for the love of God!" and threw myself at the tawny-haired Hollywood *Herald* girl, John Sixtus' daughter.

At the same instant, that big brown-furred monkey landed on the top of my living room table and grabbed up the vicious little roscoe which I'd wrenched from the tawny-haired girl's hand a moment before.

My shoulder crashed into the girl; knocked her sprawling on the floor. I went down on top of her, shielding her with my body, pinning her with my weight. She squirmed —

And at that split-second, the big brown monkey raised that little roscoe and pulled its trigger! There was a flash of yellow flame, a barking report. I felt hot lead slugging into the fleshy part of my thigh — a lead slug that had been intended for the tawny-haired girl.

Dave Donaldson, said: "God!" and fired from the hip. His bullet smashed into the monkey's skull. The animal collapsed in a bloody heap on the tabletop.

Then I yelled: "Grab that wop — quick!"

Donaldson whirled toward the organ-grinder. The dago backed off, snarling. He had an automatic in his fist. He said: "If anybody moves, I'll kill him!"

His back was toward me. I gathered my aching muscles, leaped upright from the prone form of the tawny-haired girl. I lashed myself forward, full at the organ-grinder's back.

My right arm smashed into his elbow. His automatic went skittering. And then one of Dave Donaldson's men put a hot slug through the grind-organ man's guts. The dago went down, writhing. His face punched the floor.

I leaped for him, snatched at his black wig. It came away in my hands, disclosing bright yellow hair. I rolled him over, smeared away the grease-paint on his cheeks. I said: *"Well, Mr. Konrad Vincennes,* I guess that's that!"

Vincennes looked at me with rapidly-glazing eyes.

Dave Donaldson was gasping. "What the hell is this all about, Turner?" he roared.

I said: "Vincennes murdered Ysobel LeSage. My guess is that he was jealous because she'd thrown him over in favor of John Sixtus, her boss at N-D-N Studios. Vincennes, planning to kill Ysobel LeSage, engaged me to protect her. But that was a stall. He wanted to pin the killing on Sixtus, whom he hated. He tried to time everything so I'd see Sixtus coming out of Ysobel LeSage's house right after the death-shot was fired. He figured that I would therefore be the chief witness against Sixtus!"

Donaldson said: "I still don't get it!"

I said: "Vincennes had it all planned out. He had trained a large monkey to fire a small revolver at a woman's figure — any woman. He knew John Sixtus would be visiting Ysobel LeSage this afternoon at five. Disguised as an Italian hand-organ man, Vincennes stood outside the

LeSage house, permitted the monkey to climb in the LeSage front window. The monkey, according to its training, shot Ysobel LeSage, dropped the revolver and returned to Vincennes, its master.

"John Sixtus, seeing Ysobel LeSage dead at his feet, ran out of the house. That's when I arrived at the scene. Proof that the monkey did the killing has just been demonstrated — plenty! The animal saw that roscoe on my table just now, grabbed it and fired at John Sixtus' daughter, here."

Dave Donaldson went to his knees beside the prone form of the disguised Konrad Vincennes. Vincennes was dying, and he knew it. That police slug had torn out his guts . . . Donaldson said: "Have you any statement to make, Vincennes?"

The Rumanian tenor gasped out: "Mr. Turner — is right — in all — that he has — said. I — confess. . . ." Then his eyes closed wearily; and his soul went to join that of Ysobel LeSage, the woman he had loved — and killed.

Dave Donaldson looked at me. "How did you know that Vincennes was the organ-grinder?" he asked me slowly.

I said: "It suddenly dawned on me that I hadn't left my name or address with anybody in the Italian section when I was searching for the hand-organ man who'd played outside the LeSage house. In fact, nobody knew I was looking for the organ-grinder — nobody except Vincennes himself! He was the only one to whom I'd told my plans. Yet the organ-grinder came here to my apartment. That's what gave Vincennes away — only I was too dumb to see it until almost too late!"

Donaldson turned to his men. "Grab this dead guy and that monkey, boys," he said. "We'll get out of here and leave Turner alone. He looks like he needs some rest."

So they went out. And then the tawny-haired daughter of John Sixtus crept toward me "Mr. T-Turner — Dan . . . " she whispered. "You — you saved my life and you cleared my father!" Then, suddenly, she saw blood trickling through my pants-leg, where the monkey's bullet had nicked my thigh . . . *"You're hurt!"* she gasped.

"A little," I admitted.

"I — I'll bandage it for you . . ." she said.

I grinned. My thigh-wound was just a scratch; it didn't hurt a hell of a lot. But I pretended I was in agony. I said: "I'm going to need a nurse to stay with me all night, baby. Have you got any other engagements?"

She blushed. For the first time, she remembered that her blouse was torn and her breasts were bare She covered them with her hands. Then she said: "I — I'll stay here with you, if . . . if you want me to. . . ."

I pulled her hands away from her lovely bosom. I said: "Get ready to take care of your patient, sweetness!"